**'I'm aski   ,
Max said s**

Sara froze. 'What did you say? Are you drunk?' she gasped.

'Not in the least.'

'Why?'

'I'm into my mid-thirties, I'm tired of playing the field and I need a wife.' Which still left the real question unanswered.

'But why me?'

'You're honest. You're loyal, you're bright, and beautiful, and I find you very desirable. I mistrust love matches. I'm not an emotional man, and from what I've seen of others love usually turns into a bad joke.'

Sara was lost for words…

Jane Donnelly began earning her living as a teenage reporter. When she married the editor of the newspaper she freelanced for women's magazines for a while, and wrote her first Mills & Boon® romance as a hard-up single parent. Now she lives in a roses-round-the-door cottage near Stratford upon Avon, with her daughter, four dogs and assorted rescued animals. Besides writing she enjoys travelling, swimming, walking and the company of friends.

MAX'S PROPOSAL

BY
JANE DONNELLY

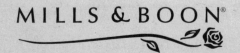

MILLS & BOON®

First published in Great Britain 1998
Harlequin Mills & Boon Limited,
Eton House, 18-24 Paradise Road, Richmond, Surrey TW9 1SR

© Jane Donnelly 1998

ISBN 0 263 80749 5

Set in Times Roman 11½ on 12 pt.
02-9804-45986 C1

Printed and bound in Great Britain
by Mackays of Chatham PLC, Chatham

CHAPTER ONE

SARA SOLWAY'S toes felt red-hot in the pretty pumps with the rhinestone heels. So much for that bargain. Marked down in the sales, she hadn't been able to resist them. Now if she didn't get out of them soon she would be needing scissors to cut them off because she could feel her feet puffing up. Music and voices filled the air from the Bonfire Night Ball in the great hall of the Moated House, but there was no one else in this corridor. Sara leaned against a door and balanced on one leg. But then the door swung inwards and sent her sprawling backwards into the room.

For a few seconds she lay winded on the carpet. Lights and noise spilled in from the corridor; behind her the shadowy room was quiet. She sat up, easing off her shoes, which felt wonderful. She was not going back straight away. She wouldn't be missed for a while. She was on duty tonight, covering the ball for the local newspaper. Carrying her shoes, she padded between the shapes of furniture towards the long window at the far end of the room and the big wing-backed chair. She sank into the downy softness of the chair and pulled her feet up under her so that she could massage her insteps. When she went back she would get a strong black coffee to keep herself awake...

But then suddenly lights went on. She shifted slightly, flexing her shoulders, and stiffened when she recognised a man's voice. She hadn't caught the words. Realising who was speaking had brought her wide awake. Although he was the one with every right to walk into any room. It was his house. He was hosting tonight's charity ball. If anyone strolled in, switching on lights, it would probably be Max Vella. But he was about the last man Sara wanted to find her snoozing in a hidden corner. Not that it was any of his business what she did. He didn't own the *Chronicle*. Half the town maybe, but he was not her boss.

Then she heard him say, 'Right, and now I'll tell you what you're going to do.' Sara could be overhearing something top secret because he was not giving friendly advice he was issuing orders. Another man mumbled something and Vella said, 'Just listen.'

Sara was a born reporter and that meant a born listener, and she huddled down in the chair, making herself as small as possible, bright-eyed with anticipation. She could see nothing. Her chair was turned away from the room, facing the window, and that was as well because it meant they couldn't see her.

They were discussing some property that might be going at a knock-down rate, Sara gathered, and the other man was to grease palms and keep Vella's name out of it. The other man didn't sound too happy. He sounded small and anxious, while Max Vella was always big and aggressive enough to stop a tank.

She must remember every word. This could add up to a corruption exposé. The local paper she worked for would be wary of taking on one of the town's leading employers, but there were other papers and radio stations that would be interested.

They seemed to be walking away from her towards the door, because the voices were quieter until she heard Vella say, 'If he won't co-operate I want him out of the way permanently. Another accident. As soon as possible.' Sara's little glow of triumph went as abruptly as if icy water had been tipped over her. He couldn't have meant what she thought he'd meant. Everybody knew he was as ruthless as they come, but out of the way *permanently*…?

This sort of thing was part of the plot of novels and TV films. It *did* happen. But when you'd come along to cover a charity bash and overheard your host arranging a fatal accident it paralysed you. *Another* accident? How many had there been? She pressed fingertips to her temples, feeling a vein pulsing hotly beneath the thin skin. What was she going to do? Who should she tell? Who would believe her when she said she'd fallen asleep and woken to hear this? They would think she'd still been only half-awake, and with only Sara's word who would make an enemy of Max Vella?

He had the clout of big money. But somebody's life was in danger and when she got out of here she must look for who was with Vella. She would have to if he and the man were still together—although she probably wouldn't recognise the other man's voice as it had hardly been raised above a murmur.

She was breathing fast and shallowly, like a cornered animal. There had been silence since she'd heard the door close. They had surely been gone long enough for her to creep out and hurry back into the cover of the crowds, but she couldn't move a muscle. She was punch-drunk, shocked rigid and she felt him before she saw him.

His shadow seemed to fall over her and then he was beside the chair, looming over her. 'Well, hello,' he said. 'What have we here?'

Instinctively and frantically she tried to grin, stretching her lips in a grimace that might pass as a smile, gibbering, 'Oh, *hello*; this is a wonderfully comfortable chair. It's a dreadful thing to say but I fell asleep for a few minutes. Not that this isn't a brilliant party, but my shoes were pinching so I kicked them off and closed my eyes.' She looked at her wrist-watch, and he must see how her hand was shaking. 'Am I in time for the fireworks?'

'You haven't missed the fireworks,' he said. 'You haven't missed a thing.'

He knew what she had heard and she couldn't get out of here. She couldn't pass him; he was too big, too strong. She couldn't scream either because her throat was closing up.

'Not very observant, are you?' he said.

'Huh?' What was he talking about?

'Second frame along.' He pointed to the window wall. 'That, my little newshound, is a mirror.'

In a heavy gilt frame was a large lacquered painting of red goldfish among dark weeds. It looked Oriental, and you could easily imagine that the fish were swimming, the weeds swaying. Among several pictures, Sara hadn't even glanced at it before, but the background was a mirror and she could see how it would reflect anyone sitting in the wing-backed chair.

'When did you see me?' The words jerked through her dry lips.

'About a minute into the conversation I looked across and there was this sharp little face peering between the weeds.' He sounded amused, and she choked.

'You recognised me?'

'I've got very good eyesight. Yes, I recognised the redhead from the *Chronicle*.'

He must have eyes like a hawk, but Sara's hair *was* bright. Looking into the mirror background now, she saw her own worried face, her hair the colour of the lacquered goldfish, and the tall, dark figure of the man beside her. She couldn't turn and face him but she couldn't take her eyes off his reflection.

'You'd no business being in here,' he went on. 'And what you heard doesn't amount to a row of beans. I'm interested in some real estate, but if I make an offer in my name the price goes up. I'm using a middleman, and so what? But, going by your beady eyes and the way your nose was twitching, you thought you'd got yourself a nice little scoop.'

He had been making a fool of her, and he was

laughing at her now. 'Did you both see me?' she asked.

'He's short-sighted. He didn't see you and he wasn't in the room towards the end, but I wondered how you'd react if you thought you'd hit the lottery. You couldn't believe your ears at first, could you? I saw you shaking your head. Then you decided it was for real. You actually believed I was knocking off the competition.'

She said sharply, 'Of course I didn't.'

'Of course you did. You were scared silly.'

She was relieved of course that he had been play-acting, but it had made her feel ill, and she snapped, 'Of course I was shocked; I was appalled.'

'It's appalling that you were stupid enough to credit it.'

She jumped out of the chair to round on him, resentment bubbling up in her. 'Why shouldn't I believe it? For all I know you could be ordering accidents like hot dinners, and it was a stupid thing to do. I nearly had a heart attack.'

'Serves you right,' he said. 'Skulking in corners, snooping.' He tutted at her as if she were a pushy child.

When she said coldly, 'I am a journalist,' he grinned.

'Not much of a one if you're gullible enough to believe somebody would brief a hit man without making damn sure no one else was listening.'

But the room had been in darkness and must have seemed empty, and she was not as sharp as usual. Last night almost without sleep had dulled her wits, and belatedly she tried for a little dignity. 'I was asleep in here. I woke up when you came in so I didn't have that much time to clear my head.'

The top of her head reached halfway up his chest. Tall and powerfully built, he towered over her, and she needed the extra inches her high heels would give her. One shoe was right there and she shoved her foot into it, looking round for its mate.

'I hope I can walk in these,' she babbled. 'It's a mistake to take your shoes off if your feet get hot. I did it in a cinema once.' Sara tended to jabber when she was nervous but not usually as badly as this.

The second shoe was under the footstool and as she kicked it out she swayed slightly. He need not have supported her and when he put a hand under her elbow it did more harm than good, startling her off-balance almost into his arms. And that was when the door opened and a couple took a couple of steps into the room. They both stared, gasped and backed out fast, pulling the door to behind them. Still holding Sara, Max Vella burst out laughing.

'The question is,' he said, 'whether they think I'm assaulting you or we're both enjoying this.'

She must have looked dishevelled to the pair who had just walked in, but it was such a mad idea that she and Max Vella were up to anything. And even crazier that he would be forcing himself on her. Sara couldn't hold back a giggle.

She knew Vella, of course. She had met him at local functions where he was always a focus of attention. As he was anywhere. He was well over average height with a hard man's good looks and the potent charisma of someone who had fought his way through rough times to come out right at the top.

She had also been in his arms before. Once. At a Lord Mayor's ball when someone had bet her she wouldn't dare ask him to dance, and Sara had taken the three paces that divided them and asked before she had given herself time to think. Then she had been in the middle of the dance floor with Vella as her partner, and he had said, 'No comment, to whatever you're going to ask next.'

He never gave interviews. He had thought that had been what she was after, and she'd said, 'Would I ask you to dance for an interview?'

'You would,' he'd said. That near to him, she had been able to see how the sensual mouth curved when he smiled. There had been butterflies in her stomach and she'd quipped back, 'I've just been dared to ask you. I have a very small bet riding on this.'

'Not too small, I hope.' He had been amused but she had begun to feel stupid. He was a stunningly sexy man but he was too rich and too strong for Sara.

Usually she was a good dancer but she had been dancing awkwardly then, wanting the music to stop. When it had he'd let her go at once and she'd backed off fast.

Now she was in his arms again, and this time she noticed the little lines that radiated from the corners of his eyes. He had hooded eyes, but she could see they were gun-metal grey, glinting with laughter, and the strength of him was overpowering enough to weaken her bones.

She croaked, 'Shouldn't we follow that couple and explain?'

'Explain what?'

That they were going off with completely the wrong idea. But Sara wouldn't know how to begin to explain so that had been a silly suggestion. If they gossiped it couldn't matter to her. Almost certainly Max Vella wouldn't care less what gossips said about him. He was no longer holding her, and she sat down on the footstool to ease her foot into the second shoe.

Vella had taken a chair too. 'Thank you,' he said, and that brought her head up with a jerk.

'What for?'

'For livening up the evening.' She supposed she had given him a couple of laughs, what with this and the hit man.

'Don't tell me you were getting bored?' she said sweetly.

'I was not the one who fell asleep. You must have been bored to death.'

She was not expected to doze off when she was sent out to cover one of the top social occasions of the year. 'I was tired,' she said defensively.

'You look healthy enough.' He gave her a slow head-to-toe scrutiny and she found herself crossing her arms over her breasts as if she were covering

nakedness, although her dress was perfectly ad-
equate.

Of course she looked healthy. She was healthy.
She had a slim, strong body and a clear complexion
that looked even healthier than usual because she
was flushing slightly under his stare. 'How come
the sudden lack of stamina?' he enquired.

She snapped, 'Lack of sleep last night.'

As she said it she realised how that could sound,
and when he drawled, 'Congratulations, is he here
tonight?' the blood burned even hotter on her
cheekbones.

'I was kept awake last night by four-year-old
twins.'

Vella's eyebrows rose. 'Yours?'

He didn't know much about her, except that she
was the redhead from the *Chronicle*. Over the years
they had had a few skirmishes. Once her paper had
had to print an apology to him when Sara had mis-
read her notes reporting a quote of his. But he had
never shown any interest in her personally. She
could be married or a single parent for all he knew.
'They're my sister's,' she said. 'They were staying
at my place last night and they ate half a pound of
chocolate truffles between them.'

'You sound about as useful a babysitter as you
are a reporter.'

She prided herself on being accurate and consci-
entious in her work—that slip-up had been years
ago—and she snapped, 'How the hell would you
know what I'm like as a babysitter? I didn't give
them the chocolates. They found them after they'd

been put to bed.' Sleeping pills had kept her sister Beth deep asleep in the little bed in Sara's tiny spare room, and she had come into the kitchen this morning white-faced and heavy-eyed, as Sara had boiled a kettle for early-morning tea.

Sara had explained that the twins had passed a sickly night but were sleeping now, and Beth had said, 'Wouldn't you know it? I'm sorry, Sar, but we'll have to go back. I know what you're going to say and you're right, of course, but I can't help loving him.'

It was no more than Sara had expected. 'Can't help loving that man' seemed to be the curse of the Solway women. Not Sara, but both her sister and her mother.

Head down now, Sara fumbled with her shoe, her hair veiling her face so Max Vella couldn't see the shadow that crossed her face. She had had plenty of practice at hiding her personal problems, and when he said, 'You didn't finish the story of taking your shoes off in the cinema,' she looked up and forced a smile.

'I got them on again. It wasn't easy but I hobbled out and snapped at the man I was with and he never asked me for another date.'

'And you never asked him?'

She pulled a face, 'If he couldn't handle a little thing like that I couldn't see much of a future for us.'

'And you're not a girl who does a lot of snapping?'

'I do not. I have a very sweet nature.'

'Now why don't I find that tallies with what I know of you?'

'I wouldn't know why.' She put on a look of injured innocence. 'Unless, maybe, you bring out the worst in me.'

Whether he was roaring with laughter or chuckling, as he was now, his laughter sounded genuine. Tonight she liked his laughter. And she quite liked the way his crisp dark hair curled back from his forehead and round his ears. In a superbly tailored evening suit, white silk shirt and black tie, he was the lord of this manor house. But she'd heard he had started off locally on a market stall and had gone on from there with the devil's own luck.

She blurted, 'You started on the markets, didn't you?' She should be trying for an interview.

'That was another life,' he said.

'I'd love to hear about it.'

'I'm sure you would.'

She was never going to get a chance like this again—a tête-à-tête with Max Vella, him thanking her for brightening his evening. She took a deep breath and pleaded, 'It wouldn't hurt you, would it, to talk to me? It would be a scoop for me and I'm sure you don't have anything to hide.'

She was sure that he had, and that he would never incriminate himself to a reporter. But her editor would be glad of any entertaining copy of the local tycoon with the Midas touch who never gave interviews. Starting with whether he was from gypsy stock. That was one of the rumours, and it could be a talking point.

'You're an opportunist,' said Vella.

She had overheard him making a business arrangement just now and he thought she was using that as a gentle persuader. But he still seemed amused, and she said, 'Takes one to know one,' astonishing herself at her own cheek.

'I'll consider it.' He was going to give her something to publish. She had an entrée here, and a lousy day was becoming surprisingly special. He sat down in one of the other chairs. 'Now tell me about yourself,' he said. He leaned back, arms folded, hooded eyes fixed on her, and she would have liked to get up off the footstool and sit in a chair herself. She was not too happy down here, crouching at his feet. It was flattering in a way, him being prepared to listen to her talking about herself, but he was probably the toughest man she had ever come across and she was going to have to watch what she told him.

'Have you worked anywhere else but the *Chronicle*?' he asked her.

'I was taken on as a trainee journalist there and when I qualified I joined the staff.'

'That's it? No urge to move on?' He must always have been hungry for success. He wouldn't understand how anyone could stay in the same smallish job for years, and she had been with the *Chronicle* for over four years.

He made her feel a real stick-in-the-mud, and she said loftily, 'Of course, I've got ambitions. I'm not planning on staying put till I draw my pension.'

The door opened again, the sound of voices drifting in, and Max stood up. 'Can I help you?' he said curtly.

'Just looking around,' trilled a woman. 'It is all right, isn't it?'

'Not in here.'

Sara peeked round the side of the chair and heard the large lady in blue velvet say, 'Pardon the intrusion,' eyes popping at Sara as she turned to leave.

'That was the mayoress,' said Sara, as if he didn't know.

'That,' he said, 'is a nosy old bat who didn't believe what she was told and came to see for herself.'

The town's mayoress was a great one for gossip, and hearing that Max Vella was wrestling in here with the local reporter would be a juicy item.

'This is crazy,' said Sara.

'You didn't help much. You could have stood up instead of peering up from floor level.' He was grinning again. She had leaned sideways from the footstool to look round the chair so that it might have seemed she was lying on the floor. 'Is some man with a claim on you likely to be barging in next to get you out of my clutches?' he asked.

'There's nobody here with a claim on me.'

'I'm glad to hear it.' Which meant of course he was glad there wouldn't be another silly scene, rather than pleased there was no man at the centre of Sara's life right now. The idea of anybody she knew standing up to Max Vella was extremely unlikely, but perhaps she ought to be getting out of here. She badly wanted to interview him but she was not so keen about him cross-questioning her. She had her shoes on. They were still tight and she took one off again and tried flexing it.

'Why come to a dance in shoes that don't fit?' he enquired.

'They felt fine earlier. They felt all right when I bought them; I got them in a sale last week and they seemed such a bargain.'

'You get what you pay for,' he said.

'That's rich, coming from you. You were setting up a bargain just now, weren't you, that sounded like a very dodgy deal?'

He shrugged that off. 'Life's a dodgy deal. It's a tough world.'

She couldn't argue there, and she looked ruefully at her 'bargain'. 'Mostly,' she said, 'you get what you can afford, or have you forgotten how that was?'

'I don't forget much.'

For a moment she almost felt as if they could swap hard-luck stories, which was ridiculous when his luck was brilliant and he had everything, including a house that Sara had always loved. Vella had lived locally in the penthouse of a riverside block of apartments he owned, before he had moved into the Moated House. When he'd bought this place he had spent a fortune on renovations, but he was not a man Sara could imagine permanently settling anywhere, and she asked him, 'Shall you stay here?'

'Probably. I've been here now for—' He paused to work out dates.

She said promptly, 'Five years and nearly five months.'

'That's about right.'

'That's dead right. I remember you moving in. Mid-June and blazing hot.' She could recall it vividly and there was a far-away look in her eyes. 'We lived at Eddlestone then. I had a horse and I used to ride over the hills and I saw the vans below. I often came this way just to look down at the house.'

'You did?' That seemed to surprise him.

She said, 'Well it's a fantastic place, isn't it, with its history and all? Some days when it's raining or there's dew on the grass you can imagine the moat's still there. The buildings can't have changed much, the towers and the bridge. You are so lucky to be living here.'

'I was fourteen when I walked over the hills and saw it for the first time,' he said. 'And I promised myself that one day I'd have it.'

'Did you believe you would?'

'I always keep promises I make to myself.' He smiled, but even if he used to be dirt poor he must always have felt that nothing was beyond him.

'How about promises you make to others?' she teased.

'Now, that depends.'

They were both smiling now, and she asked him, 'What were you doing when you were fourteen?'

'Getting an education in a tough world. What were you doing when you weren't riding your horse?'

Riding her horse had been part of the pampered

life of her teens. 'Getting an education that wasn't going to be much use in a tough world,' she said.

'You seem to be coping.'

'Oh, I manage well enough,' she said airily. 'I can even get into my bargain shoes.' She stretched a slim ankle, although her foot felt puffy, and the rhinestone heels glittered.

'They look good,' he said.

'Could be diamonds.'

'Very flash. The heels alone had to be worth the money.' For a moment they sat, saying nothing, with an antique French clock ticking softly on a rosewood side table. Then he said, 'Ten to ten; we'd better get moving.'

The bonfire was lit at ten, followed by the fireworks, and if Max Vella missed the highlight of the evening everybody would be looking for him. As it was most of the company must have heard by now that he and the girl from the *Chronicle* were carrying on behind a closed door.

Vella pulled back a bolt on the long window and it became a door leading out onto lawns. 'We can walk round to the courtyard from here,' he said.

Some of the gardens had lamps burning and coloured lights in the trees, but out here there was only moonlight. There was no one else walking, and this way they would avoid the crowds in the house. The grass was velvet-soft and her thin high heels were digging into the springy turf, so that was one reason for taking off her shoes and going barefoot.

On the fifth of November bonfires dotted the sky-line with bright orange beacons, and zooming rockets and scattering stars from other parties lit up the skies. 'Tonight's the night for wishing on a star,' she said.

'There are enough of them about.'

'But with so many how would you know which was the right one?'

'That is the problem. Knowing the right one.'

'Isn't it always?' She sounded wistful. As a child she had wished on shooting stars. Little things had worked sometimes, such as wishing for a fine day for a picnic or a ring with a pink pearl in it. But the big wish that mummy wouldn't cry any more had never come true so that, even when she had been very young, Sara had stopped believing in magic.

Beyond a row of trees the lawns dipped into a grassy ditch that had once been a stretch of the moat. Coming round the house, they were reaching a gravel path, and as she leaned against a wall to put on her shoes again Max Vella swung her up off her feet into his arms as easily as if she were a child.

Surprise took her breath away. Her instinct was to shriek, but she found she was laughing. 'This is very obliging,' she said. 'Do you do this for all your guests?'

'Only those who can't get their shoes on,' he said.

They were both smiling now, sharing a joke that nobody else could understand. She was getting quite a buzz from that, and the clean, cold smell of his aftershave was intoxicating. She breathed it in, the tip of her nose against his cheek. His skin looked smooth but she could feel a slight prickle where a beard might grow.

She looped one hand round his neck. '"Please to remember the Fifth of November",' she said gaily, and knew she would never forget this one. In her wildest dreams, or nightmares, she had never envisaged herself being carried away by Max Vella. He wouldn't stumble. She was relaxed, treating this as a joke, and that was the way it had to be.

Until she had collided, as it were, with Max Vella, tonight had been work. She had been in no mood for partying. But now she was having fun, and when they left the gravel path and he continued to carry her over smoother flagstones, right into the courtyard, she made no move to get down.

Among the crowds they were the star turn so far this evening, and Sara was getting a fit of giggles at all the surprised faces turned towards them. As guests stepped aside for their host and his burden, she kept one arm round his neck and dangled her shoes in the other hand. A woman who owned several exclusive fashion shops right out of Sara's price range asked, 'Hurt your foot, dear?'

Sara said brightly, 'Shoe trouble.'

'How very convenient.' The woman gave a sly smirk.

Max said, 'It was my pleasure.'

'You might have put that differently,' Sara whispered in his ear.

'My very great pleasure,' he said.

'They still don't think that meant what you meant.'

'Do you care what others think? Would it bother you, getting talked about?'

A few of the guests would be watching the fireworks display from windows, but it was a dry evening and almost everyone had come outside, where a throng of onlookers was circling the high structure of kindling and fuel that would soon blaze into the bonfire. Everybody seemed to be chattering, and the main topic would be that not only had Max Vella had a very private session with what's-her-name from the local paper but he hadn't been able to keep his hands off her long enough to put her down and let her stand on her own feet.

The bonfire went up with a marvellous whoosh as Max gently put Sara down. Then they stood and watched the wonderful display of fireworks. Some of the time she held onto his arm, sometimes he put an arm around her, but they stayed linked together. The last rocket of all was the most spectacular, throwing out star after star which fell away until the final burst of white light, the biggest and the best, rose in the sky so high it seemed to be vanishing. Then it fell, like a great shooting star, to a chorus of delighted gasps.

Sara turned to Max. 'That has to be the star for wishing on.'

'So are you wishing?'

'Are you?'

'I don't do much wishing.'

'You don't have much left to wish for.'

'When I see something I want,' he said softly, 'I promise myself.' Like the Moated House…

With fingertips he brushed her hair back from her forehead out of her eyes and she felt the shock of it like a body blow, because the gesture seemed as intimate as if his hand had been on her breast and he had kissed her full on the lips.

He was looking down at her. One heavy eyebrow was broken by a thin white scar that gave it a devilish quirk in the flickering glow of the fire. His eyes were so dark they were unreadable, and her mouth went dry because suddenly she had no doubt at all of his meaning. Max Vella wanted her…

CHAPTER TWO

MAX VELLA was not the first and he would not be
the last man to want Sara—she had always attracted
admirers. A few hours ago she could never have
imagined Max Vella fancying her. Tonight it was
possible. Surprising but possible, and she said with
mock gravity, 'What if your promise wasn't on offer?'

'That might make things more difficult.' He was
certainly coming on to her, but this was said with
a smile, not to be taken seriously, and Sara was
bubbling with laughter, all her problems forgotten
for a few hours.

When the party-goers were surging out of the
courtyard, back into the house and the buffet and
the band, Max still held her hand through his arm.
She was wearing her shoes again now, and if he
asked her to dance she would dance, but in the great
hall, at the foot of the wide oak-panelled staircase,
he asked, 'Do you want the guided tour?'

She had never seen more than the grounds and
the ground floor, when she had come here covering
charity functions. She had heard the house was
fabulous and of course she was curious. If he was
offering to show her around himself that was an
incredible bonus. 'I would like that very much,' she
said, and knew that most of the company watched

26

speechless as she and Max Vella went up the staircase together.

Up here there were lights everywhere, and the sounds of the Bonfire Night Ball reached them. Household staff occasionally flitted around but most of these rooms and corridors were empty. The Moated House had fallen on hard times when Vella had bought it but now it looked as it must have done in its glory days. Sara was entranced, and awestruck at the mighty effort and expense that must have gone into restoring the house.

The decor and furniture were perfect. Every piece seemed right for its setting, and Max Vella told her how he had acquired some of them. From private collections and salesrooms, Sotheby's, Christie's, auctions all over the country and abroad. In getting what he wanted the master of the Moated House seemed to have set himself no bounds.

When she gasped with delight at a charming pair of porcelain figures of Harlequin and Columbine he took Columbine out of the black lacquered cabinet and put it into Sara's hands. 'She's lovely,' she said.

'Chelsea red anchor period.' Whatever that was. If she had not been a collector's piece she would not have been here, but Sara wondered if he had ever looked into the exquisite little face and thought how pretty she was.

'She's lovely,' Sara said again. 'It's magic, this house. I don't know how you could ever think of leaving it.'

'Did I say I was?'

'You said you were *probably* staying.'

The scarred eyebrow lifted. 'Always the news-hound. You do remember what you hear.' He was teasing her, and she looked up from the little figurine with a slanting smile.

'If it's interesting enough, I remember.'

Flirting and fooling with Max Vella was a heady experience. When Sara got away from here she might find it hard to believe that this had been going on, although there would be plenty around to remind her. By tomorrow she would be the talk of the town for a few days. Well it was worth it. She was having a really good time—seeing the house, being flatteringly targeted by a mesmerising man and she'd almost been promised an interview. Let them talk. She had weathered worse gossip before now. 'I should be going. I'm in the office in the morning. It has been a memorable evening.'

'For me too.' He sounded like a courteous host. 'Are you driving back?'

Her little car was parked with others near a side door, which meant she didn't have to push her way through the throng and she could get away almost unnoticed. Max Vella went with her, and she wished he had not. With him standing over her, she could hardly keep her hand steady enough to get her car keys into the door lock, and then in the ignition. She did manage to say, 'You won't forget about the interview?'

'Could I?'

Of course he could. He could do anything he damn well pleased. Her gaiety ebbed away, replaced by a reaction bordering on panic. She had been playing with fire, and now she headed for town, and her own little apartment, with her heart hammering.

Her flat was over a delicatessen in the town square. She parked her car in the delivery yard and let herself into the building by a back door, into a narrow hall with a steep flight of stairs. The old red-patterned carpet was wearing thin, and the magnificent staircase in the Moated House came into her mind. Compared with that this was like climbing a ladder, and compared with that house Sara's flat was a dump.

Through the door at the top of the stairs she went into the living room where a small lamp on a side table had been left on. There were toys on the floor so Beth and the twins must still be here, and they were—all three of them lay in the same bed, the children nestling in their mother's arms.

A beam from a street lamp cast enough light to show Sara a picture that brought a lump to her throat. Her sister's dark red hair fanned out over the pillow, and long, silky lashes lay like shadows on her pale cheeks. Sleeping Beth looked hardly more than a child herself, although she was only a year younger than Sara, and the flaxen-haired children were so fragile and so vulnerable that Sara wanted to put her own arms around them all, to protect them as she always did.

'Oh, Lord, what is going to happen to you?' she whispered, and she went quietly out of the room, closing the door very gently. At least she would have a bed to herself tonight. Last night it had been the sofa and the twins' bilious turn.

She tiptoed into the bathroom, undressed and washed, making as little noise as possible. She often came back from these high-fashion affairs feeling like Cinderella, and her dress tonight had been rather special. Silky, in deep pine-green with boot-lace-thin shoulder straps, tight fitting to the low hip-line then flaring to mid-calf. With a haute couture label, although Sara had found it in an up-market jumble sale.

Most of her wardrobe came from sales and nearly-new shops, because she had to make every penny of her salary count. And she wouldn't be wearing her 'bargain' shoes again. Worry and weariness were creasing her smooth brow so that her reflection in the bathroom mirror looked older than her twenty-three years. At this rate, she thought wryly, Beth will be mistaken for my daughter before long. And it was crazy that Beth's troubles should make her seem more like a delicate child while Sara aged for both of them.

The sisters had a family resemblance in features. And both were redheads, but Beth's hair was dark auburn while Sara's flamed, and Beth's soft, pretty mouth was stronger, fuller, more sensuous in Sara. Beth faced the world with wide eyes while Sara's eyes often narrowed as she assessed the situation, and that included the men in her life. There had been men in Sara's life but she'd never taken them seriously enough for a deep relationship to develop.

A touch of mockery at the wrong time had lost her several would-be lovers.

Her reflection blurred in the mirror as a wave of fatigue swept over her. She had to get into bed before she slumped down on the bathroom floor. It was a narrow bed in the little spare room but Sara slid gratefully between cool sheets and was on the edge of sleep when a faint report brought her awake again. Somewhere they were still letting off fireworks, and her thoughts drifted back to the bonfire at the Moated House and to Max Vella standing beside her.

His arm around her shoulders had been light, but she could imagine a heavier touch crushing her so that the sheets and duvet seemed suddenly unbearably weighty. His face was in shadow that could have been a mask, and she didn't need that flash of waking nightmare interpreted. Common sense was warning her loud and clear: if he should get in touch she would have to come up with a very good reason why she couldn't see him again.

She could say that although she hadn't taken a partner to the ball she did have a lover. Someone to whom she was completely committed. Max Vella's world must be full of willing women. He wouldn't bother with the likes of Sara if she played hard to get.

He probably wouldn't get in touch because he wasn't that interested, and when she rang him about the interview he would have changed his mind about that. She tossed and turned for a few more minutes, and then fell asleep.

She would have slept longer if she had not been woken by the sound of bells ringing in her head. The sound pierced the cocoon of her slumber, and still with her eyes shut she shook her head until the ringing stopped. When she did open her eyes very slowly daylight was streaming into the room, and she would have liked to pull the sheets over her head and go back to sleep.

Her throat was dry, and she could hear the twins shrieking. She had to have a cup of coffee and a couple of aspirins or she would start the day with a thumping headache. This was a working day. She had to get into the office this morning, but first she had to find the strength to climb out of bed.

Almost at once the bedroom door opened and Beth came in with the twins skipping behind her. 'Didn't you hear the doorbell?' said Beth. 'This just came for you.' And Sara struggled to sit up, mumbling.

'What?' It was a very large box of chocolates.

'With a card,' said Beth. Written on a white card in black ink Sara read, 'No rum ruffles, try the hard centres. The interview. My office twelve midday.' And the initials M.V.

'A chauffeur brought them. Grey uniform, peaked hat, the lot. Who sent them?' Beth was agog with curiosity as Sara went on staring at the card. Sara would have recognised the writing anywhere. She couldn't remember seeing any of his writing before, but she knew he would use a thick nib and write without any flourishes. She said, 'Max Vella. I met him last night. He's giving me an interview.'

'You must have made a very good impression on him last night,' Beth said. 'I've never seen such a big box of chocolates.' It lay on the bed beside Sara, a box of fine Belgian chocolates the size of a tea tray. Josh reached for the box and his mother said, 'Don't even think about it—and how you can after those truffles.'

Sara would have to explain just what had happened before the gossip reached Beth about her sister and Max Vella. Beth would know that it was nonsense. It was quite funny, it should cheer Beth up, but Sara then realised that if she didn't hurry she'd be late for work. She would have liked to take time and trouble, fixing her hair and her make-up, choosing something smart and efficient-looking for the midday interview. Getting an interview was a fantastic stroke of luck, but she would have been happier if she hadn't been seeing him again so soon. In about a week's time would have suited her better.

Beth was still trying to persuade Sara to eat a slice of toast as Sara struggled into her coat and hurried out of the flat. Toast would have stuck in her throat. 'I don't have time for breakfast,' she called, although it was the thought of facing Max Vella again that was playing havoc with her nerves.

The offices of the *Chronicle* were across the town square from Sara's first floor flat. That had always been great—from her door to her work in less than five minutes. But it meant that this morning she shot into Reception with her coat unbuttoned, still trying to smooth down her hair.

The girl behind the counter said, 'Hello, hello, you didn't waste your time last night, did you?'

'Oh, heck.' Sara stood still and breathed deep. 'Has Carl been talking?'

There had been a *Chronicle* photographer at the ball. He must have come back with the news about Max Vella and Sara. 'Believe me,' said Sara, 'it was not what it seemed.'

A door from the front office led into the editorial department, and there she faced her colleagues, all of them waiting for her version of last night's goings-on. Trying to explain at this stage would be hopeless. She said, 'Sorry, it isn't that good a story, whatever Carl's been telling you.'

'Come off it,' Carl said huffily. He knew what he'd heard, what he'd seen. 'You were getting on with Vella like a house on fire, never mind a bonfire. And then you went off upstairs with him, just the two of you.'

'He was showing me round the house. I've never seen round it before.'

Carl hooted. 'Ha! All those rooms with four-poster beds in them.' Bedrooms had just been part of the guided tour like other rooms, but everywhere they had gone she had been conscious of the dynamic force of the man beside her.

'You went up the stairs,' Carl was declaring as if this was his proof positive. 'But nobody saw you come down again.'

'There's more than one staircase in that house,' Sara said scathingly.

Carl grinned. 'A backstairs way out? What time did you leave?'

'Before you did,' she said, and she didn't want any more of this. 'Get any good pictures?' she asked.

'I missed the best,' Carl had to admit. 'You barefoot and him carrying you into the courtyard.'

She couldn't explain that either, and the editor spoke up. 'Max Vella? We are talking about Vella?' And Sara nodded. 'Doesn't sound like him,' the editor mused.

'I wouldn't know,' Sara said wearily. 'I'll ask him when I see him again. He's giving me an interview at twelve o'clock.'

The next half-hour she spent with the editor, planning the interview. The *Chronicle* was a long-established county newspaper that rarely had anything very exciting to publish. Jim Kelly had been in this job for twenty-odd years. He was delighted that one of his staff would be interviewing the local tycoon who had never given an interview before.

'Get some human interest,' Sara was instructed. 'Where he came from, what local plans he's got.'

Like the dodgy deal I overheard, Sara might have said, when there were no names mentioned and nothing to tie it in with anything. 'Human interest,' she repeated, and Jim Kelly chuckled.

'Some say Vella isn't human but you seem to have surprised them all last night.'

'Last night was pretty surprising all round,' Sara muttered.

Afterwards she wrote captions for the pictures

Carl had taken, and an account of the ball, the charity getting the proceeds, and a list of local bigwigs who had attended. She made no mention of course of herself, although she was going to be a main topic in any discussion of last night at the Moated House.

She was beginning to regret all of it. This morning she would have given a lot to put back the clock and keep out of the darkened room so that she never came up against Max Vella or anything that happened afterwards. Watching the office clock edging round to midday, her tension was building up by the minute, and when there was a phone call for her she hoped it was Vella's office, postponing their meeting.

It was Beth. 'Are you all right?' Beth wanted to know. Assured that Sara was fine, she went on apologetically, 'I'm going to have to talk to Jeremy. He's at home and I've got to find out, well, how bad things are. Well I have, haven't I?'

Sara was resigned to this; it was the way it always happened. 'Sure,' she said. 'Get the figure and we'll talk about it.'

One thing that never surprised Sara was her brother-in-law. Jeremy Bolton was a problem and always had been. Two nights ago Beth had phoned Sara's flat in tears. 'It's happening again, he's been betting on the horses again. He's lost, of course, he always loses, but he never seems to learn. He *promised* me, and now— Oh, I've got to get away, I've got to get the twins out of here. I can't think straight; I don't know what to do. We can't go to mother's; you know how she is when she's upset. She can't listen, she can't take it in. Sar, will you fetch us?'

Since then her sister and the twins had been staying with Sara, and now Beth was on her way to a tearful reunion when Jeremy would promise everything and Beth would believe him.

Tonight Sara would be drawn into that, but first she had a confrontation with Max Vella and it was a toss-up which meeting she was dreading more. Her sister's husband was a never-ending drain on Sara's finances and energy. He depressed her, but she knew what she was dealing with with Jeremy. No surprises there.

But Max Vella was as menacing as walking into an uncharted minefield. He was always civil with the press, open-handed to charities. Sara had heard it said, 'He'll be Sir Max before he's forty, if he isn't in jail.' But she had never heard of him giving any journalist a face-to-face interview before.

She had amused him last night. He did have a cruel sense of humour. He had made her squirm with the hit man joke, scared her silly. He could be making a fool of her with this interview. She could imagine him sitting behind a huge desk, dominant and arrogant, while she perched on the edge of a small chair, stuttering her questions. He could imply as he had last night that she wasn't much of a journalist if she blew it and ended up getting no story at all.

But she was good at her job, and she had to stop undermining her self-confidence by wondering why

he had agreed to talk to her. The only important
fact was that he had, and there was no reason why
he should scare her. Well not scare her exactly but
make her apprehensive, because he was the kind of
man who overawed most people, and Sara couldn't
know what mood he would be in when she was
shown into his office.

She arrived dead on time. She didn't want to
hang around and she was not keeping him waiting.
So it was five minutes to twelve when she walked
through the revolving doors into the office block
and was taken to the top floor by a young man in
a smart suit and what could be an old school tie.

Young men usually tried to chat up Sara. This
one eyed her appreciatively but said nothing as they
travelled up in the smooth, fast-moving lift. The lift
doors opened onto an area of ash-panelled walls
and thick grey carpeting. A door was open. Sara's
guide said, 'Miss Solway, sir,' and Sara thought,
Into the lion's den, and then, Well he can't eat me,
and went in with her long-legged stride.

Her next thought, as Vella rose from his chair
behind the desk, was that he seemed even taller and
broader-shouldered today. But he seemed welcoming. She was seated, offered tea or coffee, and
started to say, 'No, thank you,' when she changed
her mind. The headache she had woken with was
still lurking. Even an affable Max Vella would be
stressful and a tea or coffee might steady her. 'I
would like a coffee,' she said.

Coffee for two was brought in by an elegant
blonde. Max Vella took his black; Sara doubted if

he went for sweetness in anything. She had sugar in hers but it was scalding when she took a sip, and that showed the state she was in because any fool could see it was steaming hot. It brought tears to her eyes as she gulped it down instead of spluttering it out, only thankful that she hadn't dropped the cup.

After a few seconds she managed to say, 'Thank you for seeing me. My editor was very pleased.'

'We aim to please,' said Vella.

She hoped, but from what she knew the one he aimed to please was usually himself. She took her pocket recorder out of her handbag and put it on the desk, switching it on and asking, 'Do you mind?'

'You don't think you're going to hear anything interesting enough to remember?'

'Oh, I'm sure I shall.' She was not sure at all.

'Or is this likely to be more reliable than your notes?' He had to be harking back to the time when Sara had given the impression he was turfing somebody out of a cottage when he had been doing no such thing, and the paper had had to print an apology in the next edition.

She snapped, 'You don't forget, do you? I was a student then; I've learned a lot since.' And suddenly he was smiling and it was more like it had been last night.

'So where do we start?' he said, and she went quickly into her first question.

'Anything you can tell our readers about your local plans? Such as the cinema?'

A supermarket near the town centre had closed down and options for the site were being considered. There was talk of a group of businessmen with Vella at their head building a cinema. 'What do you think?' he asked her. 'Is there a demand? The last cinema closed down.'

The *Chronicle* had printed letters from the public and Sara had done a street quiz asking the opinions of passers-by. This was a tourist town with a theatre. Most visitors and most of the locals would welcome the extra entertainment. 'The old cinema was years ago,' she said. 'I'm sure a new one would do well this time.'

'You'd patronise it?'

'Yes, I would.'

'What are your favourite films?'

They discussed a few films—what she had seen recently, which she had enjoyed, which had bored her, which had made her think. It was such a relief to find him easy to talk to. She asked, 'What were you doing here when you walked over the hills and first saw the Moated House?'

He told her. 'Working with a travelling fair. I was one of the strong-arm gang who put up and dismantled the heavy rides.'

This was lovely stuff, and she recalled something else he had said last night. 'You were only fourteen when you were doing this?'

'I looked older. Big for my age and a good liar.'

'And then?'

'I started in the scrap-metal business, got a small yard in Yorkshire, went on the markets up and down the country, buying, selling, one thing leading to another.'

It sounded easy but it must have been a killing struggle, and she said with real admiration, 'From small-time huckster to tycoon was a magnum leap.'

'A step at a time.'

'Why did you leave the fair?'

'Time to move on. And there was a fight.' His smile made her smile. 'Bordering on a brawl.'

She tried to imagine him younger, hungrier, a scrapper, and couldn't. The boy and the man were a world apart. His hands were smooth, the nails manicured, but they were strong enough to be a fighter's hands, and she wondered when he had stopped using brute force because his brain was a deadlier weapon.

She asked, 'Did you get that scar in the brawl?' She was feeling confident enough to ask, as if they were on their way to being friends.

But he said, 'I got it in the road accident that killed my parents.'

And she cringed at her lack of sensitivity, stammering, 'I'm so sorry.'

'It was a long time ago,' he said. 'Now tell me about yourself.' And somehow the conversation reverted back to Sara.

She didn't mind. She answered everything he asked about her job, her likes and dislikes, although it did seem more as if he were interviewing her than the other way round. It was when he said, 'Which was your house when you lived in Eddlestone?' that she became uneasy.

She said abruptly, 'The Grange, next to the church. That was a long time ago too.'

He nodded. 'You were Geoffrey Solway's daughter.' But she was not discussing her father with him. Max Vella had been here when Geoffrey Solway had died but Vella had always been in a much higher league. There had been no business dealings between them. If they had met it had been casually. That part of Sara's life was no concern of Max Vella, and she resented him dragging it into this—interrogation.

She was realising now that was the word for how the interview was going. She was being interrogated. She had been beguiled into believing this was a friendly meeting, but he had questioned her far more than she had been permitted to question him. 'Where are you living now?' he asked her.

She said, 'In a very small flat in the square. You're not the only one to make a quantum leap. Only yours was up and mine was down.'

A phone on the desk rang. Saved by the bell, she thought, and picked up her tape recorder. When she was calmer she would play it back and see what she could dig out.

'I'll be with you,' Vella said into the phone, and to Sara, 'We'll continue this later. This evening over dinner. I'm thinking of offering you a job. I'll collect you at your flat at seven-thirty p.m.'

'Don't bother,' she said. She heard the words come out of her mouth but he didn't seem to. He was glancing through a sheaf of papers he had taken out of a drawer, and the sharp-suited young man appeared at Sara's elbow as suddenly as a genie popping out of a bottle. Max Vella could turn up where he liked at seven-thirty Sara decided; she would be anywhere but the flat.

The young man saw her down in the lift and the commissionaire touched the peak of his hat in salute as she left the building. She sat in her car, fingers clenched, trying to quell a surge of frustration.

There were several expensive cars in the car park and if she had to guess which was Vella's she would pick the silver-grey Mercedes—it looked like his kind of car. Sara had a real urge to scratch the gleaming paintwork. He had annoyed and disturbed her. Bringing up her family background was probably no more than the bluntness of a man who never had to consider anyone else's feelings, but it had hit a raw nerve in Sara. She was over-sensitive today with Beth going back to Jeremy, and the problem would be waiting for Sara: how much the bookies had let Jeremy run up this time.

Beth would be phoning Sara or coming to the flat, and when Sara found the door at the top of the stairs unlocked she half expected to find Beth and Jeremy sitting in her living room, both looking woebegone and very young. Jeremy was another one who never seemed to age. He and Beth could pass as teenagers but Sara felt very old indeed.

The living room was empty, and she called, 'Hello,' getting no reply. There was no one in the kitchen, and the bathroom door was ajar. Nobody in there either.

She called again, 'Hello, Beth,' lifting the latch

on her bedroom door. She couldn't get in because the bolt had been slipped in there, and for a second she thought resentfully, They could have stayed in their own home to make up. But of course they would have done. And then she heard a little choking sound, like a strangled whimper.

The children could have done it, if they had been left alone for a few minutes. She spoke through the narrow space edging the door that didn't fit too well. 'Jo, Josh, are you in there? Pull the bolt back. You can do it. Just pull it along.' There was silence, and she spoke louder. 'Who *is* in there?' Rapping with her knuckles, 'Can you hear me?'

Nobody answered; something was very wrong. She beat on the door again, shouting, 'Answer me.' When no one did she was turning away—she had to get in, maybe with a ladder to the window—then she heard the click of the bolt sliding back. She lifted the latch and pushed the door, and Beth stood there swaying, her eyes glazed and little white pills slipping through her nerveless fingers.

CHAPTER THREE

SARA caught Beth as she slumped to the floor and staggered with her to the bed. Beth's head fell back, her mouth was open, there were pills on her tongue, and when Sara put fingers into her mouth she gagged and heaved.

'How many?' Sara's voice was hoarse and Beth wasn't hearing. A bottle of pills was half-empty. A few more pills were scattered on the bedside table with an empty glass and a vodka bottle. Beth was no drinker—a couple of glasses of wine could get her giggling and silly, and spirits always brought on one of her migraines—but Sara was praying she only had a hangover to deal with here. When Beth's eyelids fluttered Sara hissed in her ear, 'How many pills have you taken?'

'I swallowed some, I think,' Beth whimpered.

'Not those that were in your mouth.' Sara shook her gently but insistently. 'Don't go to sleep. Wake up. Come on Bethie.' She heaved her sister into the sitting position. 'Talk to me; what are you *doing*? It's going to be all right, whatever's happened; I promise you, Bethie.'

She rushed to the kitchen to switch on the kettle and scoop spoonfuls of instant coffee into a mug. Then back to Beth, who was still sitting up on the bed with her head dropping onto her knees, moaning, 'Oh, God, I feel awful.'

'Of course you do,' Sara howled. Beth had come to the door with a fistful of pills. Sara had scooped three of them off her tongue and now she worked frantically, getting strong coffee down her.

'Come on, Bethie, there's a good girl, it's going to be all right.' Beth's fuddled mind cleared enough for her to assure Sara that the sleeping pills in her mouth were the first she had taken.

'Where are the children?' Sara had been so caught up in the horror of finding Beth like this there had been no time to think of anything else, but for a moment now she was terrified.

When Beth whispered, 'I left them with Maureen before I went home,' Sara breathed a prayer of relief. Maureen was a friend and neighbour of Beth's, a sensible, middle-aged woman. The children would be safe with her.

She had Beth stumbling around, drinking water now, and slowly coming out of the anaesthetic of alcohol into the despair that had made her lock herself in that room.

When Sara asked, 'Why?' Beth began weeping. 'It's over.'

'Has Jeremy left you?' Sara thought that could only be a blessing.

But Beth said, 'Of course not. But this time there's no hope at all.' She sat down on the little sofa in the living room, hugging herself and rocking to and fro. 'There are men after him, money lenders and that, who are going to half kill him, and then at work—' Jeremy worked at an estate agent's in town '—there's big money trouble there. He's got till the end of the month to pay it back and he can't, and he's going to end up in prison, in jail. And I can't face it, Sar.' She lifted a tear-stained, stricken face. 'If you hadn't come back early I wouldn't have had to.'

Sara's blood ran cold when she thought what she would have found if she had returned at her usual time. 'What about the children?' she demanded. 'How could you leave the children?'

'They'd have been all right. You'd have looked after them.'

Beth was a child herself, as loving and as vulnerable. Sara had always known that, and what she had to do now was make Beth see that nothing was so bad there was no hope. They couldn't find the cash to save Jeremy. Sara had no assets and her credit rating was nil, but as she racked her brain a sudden thought came like a flash of light.

She said slowly, 'Max Vella might offer me a job.' He ran an empire with countless career openings. 'This interview this morning—he ended up interviewing me, practically cross-questioning me.' All he had told her about himself was his short shift with the fun fair. Even on the subject of the cinema he hadn't said whether he was backing it or not, he had just kept her talking about herself. She said, 'We didn't finish the interview, but we're talking again this evening and it does add up. I had told him I'd leave the *Chronicle* if I got a better offer

and he said he was considering making me an offer.'

She was not sure she wanted Max Vella as her
boss. It could be awkward if he did fancy her, but
she would deal with that situation if it arose. Beth
was saying, 'That could be good couldn't it?'

'Of course it could,' said Sara, and Beth stopped
rocking to and fro and clapped a hand to her mouth,
wailing. 'I'm going to be sick.'

Sara got her to the bathroom, held her head over
the loo, then sponged her face and helped her back
to the bedroom. While Beth lay on the bed, drained
and drowsy, Sara rang their mother and told her,
'Beth has a migraine and I have to go out this evening. The twins will be in bed, but will you come
round to the flat and sit with them?'

'What are Beth and the twins doing in your flat?'
Francesca Solway never faced up to trouble if she
could avoid it but she got the message here; it was
not the first time Beth had left home. 'Oh, dear, is
Jeremy being naughty again?'

'You could say that,' Sara said ironically.

'He *is* a silly boy,' said Francesca, as if a slap
on the wrist would settle that. 'Very well,' her
mother's girlish voice was plaintive, 'but this isn't
convenient.'

Sara collected the twins and her mother. The twins
were bathed and put to bed and Francesca settled
down in the living room with a magazine. Beth had
taken aspirins for the hangover headache that would

be waiting for her in the morning, and when Sara looked in on her she was asleep.

Tonight she was even paler than usual, and Sara realised why the little porcelain Columbine in the Moated House had tugged at her heart. It was because Columbine had Beth's delicate face. They were both fragile, both would shatter unless they were handled gently, and as Sara looked down Beth opened her eyes and whispered, 'Sorry, Sar.'

Sara smiled. 'The twins are in bed; Mother's here. Are you going to tell her?'

'What's the use?' said Beth.

No use at all, Sara could have said. 'I shouldn't be too long,' she promised. She wished she did not have to go. It was safe enough to leave Beth now, but finding her sister so near the point of no return, and knowing in her heart of hearts that Beth could do this again, had sapped the strength out of Sara.

Max Vella was the last man she would have chosen to meet tonight, but at a quarter past seven she let herself out of the building. Her mother presumed she was off on a reporting assignment. Sara did not want her thinking this was a date with Max Vella because it was not. It was, as he had said, a continuation of an interview that Sara was hoping might lead to a better job on a higher salary. So she would meet him and answer any questions that were not intimately personal.

She saw his car as she came out onto the street. It was parked across the square—it had to be the silver-grey Mercedes she had picked out earlier in the car park of his office block. The square was full of pedestrians but he must have been watching out for her because he got out of the car and she saw him crossing towards her, head and shoulders above the crowds.

She found herself with her back pressed against the door she had just closed. She could not go to meet him. The crowds seemed to move out of his way. She was probably imagining that, but her bones felt weak and she knew that if she stepped out the slightest push could send her staggering. She almost resented his strength. Why should he be so confident, so sure of himself, when she felt like death?

'Are you all right?' he said when he reached her.

'Never better.' If he caught hold of her and made her look straight at him she had an awful feeling that he would see tears behind her eyes. She made herself smile without looking at him, asking brightly, 'Where are we going?'

'The Grosvenor?'

'Lovely.' Where else? On the river, and the best hotel in town. They could have walked there in ten minutes but he was opening the car door for her, and she sank into the deep leather seat.

Listening to the soft purr of the engine as he pulled out into the traffic, she quipped, 'Why doesn't my old banger sound like this?'

She clamped her teeth on her lower lip because if she let herself go on babbling goodness knew what nonsense she would be coming out with. He, of course, was the strong and silent type. And he needed to watch the road, this time on a busy Saturday evening.

When they left the car to be parked outside the big hotel with the black and gold railings Sara was telling herself that she really was all right. And she had better be because he was a dangerously sensual man and she must keep her wits about her. She could feel his touch through the thickness of her coat sleeve. It made her arm tingle and she remembered him brushing her hair from her eyes as they'd watched the bonfire.

They were shown into a private room, with a table in the window overlooking the river. She hoped he didn't have seduction in mind. Desperately pretending to be carefree, she had never felt less seductive in her life. She agreed with what the waiter and then Vella suggested from the menu. The thought of food made her nauseous, although it looked attractive when it came—red mullet fillets glistening with a scarlet jewel-clear sauce, a bowl of crisp green salad, another of vegetables in olive oil and vinegar with tiny black pieces which had to be truffles—and she managed to swallow a few mouthfuls and gulp a little wine.

They talked about the ball. 'The mayoress went with two bottles of champagne and dropped one as she was getting into the official limo,' he told her.

'I do not believe you.' Once she started she couldn't stop laughing.

'She was drenched with the stuff. You won't be seeing her in that blue plush number again.'

There were tears in Sara's eyes now, from laugh-

ter and stress, and she fumbled in her handbag for
a tissue, bringing one up and scattering pills on the
table between them. She had gathered them all up
before she'd left home but she couldn't have se-
cured the top of the container.

'Yours?' he enquired. They could have been
aspirins, sweeteners, but she answered, 'My sister's,' before she had given herself time to try bluff-
ing it out.

'Why are you carrying them around?'

She was too weary to be fencing with him. She
took the pillbox out of her handbag and began replacing the pills one by one, slowly and carefully.
Vella watched her. Even his eyes were still, fixed
on her, and when she clicked down the lid she said
bluntly, 'To stop her taking an overdose.'

'I did hear your sister's husband was in dire
straits.'

'About as dire as they come. One lot threatening
to beat him senseless, another to get him a prison
record.' She said with a brittle and spurious gaiety,
'You wouldn't care to lend me a sizeable sum?'

'You wouldn't be blackmailing me?'

He was smiling again now, with closed lips and
hooded eyes, and she didn't catch on for a couple
of seconds. How could she blackmail him? Unless
she thought what she'd overheard last night was
valuable information. She heard herself say,
'You're going to make a packet over that deal,
aren't you?'

He shook his head at her. 'You are getting into
very deep waters.'

And she could have laughed hysterically. 'I am in deep waters, I've been in deep waters for years and now they are closing over my head. But of course I'm not trying to blackmail you. Even if I could I wouldn't be that big a fool.'

He said, 'Of course not.'

She asked, 'Does Jeremy owe you?' He might. Max Vella probably had bruisers he could call on, but he said, 'I don't have bad debts.'

And that she believed. She drained her wine glass before she could ask, 'What have you heard?'

'How much he owes to some other men who don't have bad debts and wouldn't think twice about putting him in hospital as an example. Also that he's defrauded the firm he was working for. Unless he can repay that by the end of the month he'll be charged.'

She said bitterly, 'You are well informed.'

'I have my sources.'

'And of course you know all about my father.'

'Who doesn't?'

Everyone local knew that Geoffrey Solway had cheated everybody he could, and Sara would always be known as his daughter. Max could never understand Sara's problems. She said harshly, 'My father beat the rap by dying. Jeremy might not be so lucky, unless the ones who are promising to break his legs go over the top. Beth was taking an…' She couldn't bring herself to finish the sentence. 'She'd locked herself in the bedroom and that was what was waiting for me.'

'Was she expecting you? Did she know when you'd be coming back?'

'No, that's what terrifies me.'

'She has children.'

'She knew I'd look after them.'

'You've been paying off debts for years—theirs, not yours.'

He was calm, softly spoken, and her own voice became quieter. 'My mother and my sister have never knowingly harmed or cheated anyone in their lives. They're just two silly women in love. Beth adores Jeremy, my mother loved my father. Still does.'

'Why should that make you responsible?'

She took a deep breath and locked her fingers tightly together, her eyes dark with memories. 'Because I am responsible. If it hadn't been for me Beth would never have met Jeremy. I found him. I brought him home. He and Beth looked at each other and that was it—pow. Love at first sight. Everybody was thrilled for them.

'My father took to him like a son, and he is very like our father was; they could both charm the birds off the trees. Beth was always Daddy's pet so she could have been looking for somebody like her father. Well she got it in Jeremy. She kept saying she owed it all to me, and she does, poor girl. She hasn't said that for a while but it's still true. Anyhow a few months after the twins were born my father died. You know he had an engineering firm and he had been in debt up to his eyes. It never seemed to worry him; he was spending money like water till the end.

'So the firm went, the house went, everything went. Since then Jeremy has been carrying on the family tradition and so has Beth. Beth's been a doting wife, just like our mother...'

The rush of words dried up. She had never talked like this with anyone before and when he said, 'Go on,' she tried to smile.

'Do you hear a lot of confessions? You should have been a priest.'

'I don't think so.' Neither did she. 'Go on,' he said again, and she found herself speaking again.

'Just before he died he asked me to look after Beth and my mother, and I promised I would. He must have known Jeremy was like him, what could happen to Beth, and he surely knew what lay ahead for my mother. He'd had affairs but they'd stayed together, and she was a partner in the firm, signing everything he put in front of her.'

'Which makes her liable for everything.'

Sara nodded. 'She'll be in hock to the banks for ever, but to hear her talk now my father was a lovely man. Well he was and so is Jeremy.' Her shoulders were sagging under a heavy weight, facing the facts and her own part in them. 'I found Jeremy for Beth, and I should have realised what the situation was with our mother. When it was spelled out for her she turned to me and asked, ''Why did you let me do this?''.'

'What was the woman talking about? You were a child.'

'I was nineteen when he died. I knew he cheated and I knew how easily he fooled her. I was on the *Chronicle*, supposed to be a good reporter who could get at the facts. I should have checked what was going on, what he was getting her to sign. Beth was always the sweetie, I'm supposed to be the smart one.'

'Up to a point,' he said dryly. 'You haven't looked after yourself too well.'

'I haven't looked after anybody too well.' The house of cards was tumbling down and there was no way Sara could save it. 'But I still don't think I had any choice.'

'You have now,' said Vella. 'I'm offering you a choice.'

He had to mean he could help. He could, easily, but she asked, 'Why should you?'

'Do you find me repulsive?'

She was being propositioned and she jumped up, pushing the chair back, gripping the table edge with her fingertips. She had thought he fancied her, but the bluntness of this was shattering. This *was* blackmail. She looked at him, seeing a superb specimen of animal strength and probably cruelty. A man to trust? A man to fear, for sure. And she thought, I do not know if I could go through with this. What would he want of me? 'You get what you pay for', he had told her, and when he had taken his demands in full she might be left bankrupt in body and soul.

She said, with tiny pauses, 'Why—are you—asking me that?' Maybe she did find him repulsive. She did not want him to touch her.

'It has a bearing on this position I'm offering you,' he said.

Now she began talking quickly. 'I don't know how much I'd be worth as a mistress, never having been one.' She couldn't stop talking, although her teeth were chattering. 'It's not a career move I've ever considered; I'm not sure I've got the looks for it. Or the stamina.' Her hair was falling over her face in a red mist.

'You do rattle on, don't you?' He sounded amused and she hated him.

She gritted her teeth and muttered, 'It's a bad habit I have when I'm jittery, and right now I could not be more hyper-stressed.'

'The financial situation is distressing.' Now he sounded as if he was talking business. 'But I think you have every qualification.' She had never felt more humiliated, and the agony was the cost of turning him down. 'By the way,' he said, 'I'm not looking for a mistress. What I have in mind for you is that you become my wife.'

Sara froze. He had to be amusing himself at her expense again. What was his game this time? 'What did you say?' she gasped.

'I'm asking you to marry me.'

'Are you drunk?'

'Not in the least. Do sit down,' he said.

She needed to sit down. She was hanging onto the table because her legs were giving way, and she slid back into the chair. Facing him now, her mind was reeling but she managed to say, 'Why?'

'I'm into my mid-thirties, I'm tired of playing the

field and I need a wife.' Which still left the real question unanswered.

'But why me?'

'You're honest. You're loyal. You keep your word: that promise you made to your father. I'd need a wife I could trust.' He could have been describing a suitable business partner rather than a woman he wanted to marry. He went on, 'You're bright, and beautiful, and I find you very desirable. I wanted to make love to you last night.' A half-smile lifted a corner of his mouth. 'Love's the wrong word. Leave it at I wanted you last night and I want you now. I mistrust love matches. I'm not an emotional man, and from what I've seen of others love usually turns into a bad joke.'

She agreed. 'It surely does in my family.'

'You're not in a relationship now.' Since last night he must have learned that about her too. 'Were any of your affairs serious?'

'By serious,' she said tartly, 'do you mean sexual? Are you in the market for a virgin bride?'

'I meant did you consider yourself in love with any of them? You're not carrying a secret torch for a past flame?'

Love was a trap, she knew. She said, 'Even without the example of my mother and sister, do I look the sort to fall wildly in love?'

'I wouldn't have thought so, not with that jawline.' This time when he looked at her and smiled she could almost feel the touch of his fingertips tracing the contours of her face. 'Good bones,' he said, 'and marvellous skin, but that could be a stub-

born jaw. No, you do not look to me like a senti-
mental lady.'

They had to be playing a crazy game. 'How
about you, have you ever fallen *wildly*?' She
drawled 'wildly', exaggerating it, and he grinned.

'Wildly, never.' Surprise, surprise; she couldn't
see him losing control of his emotions or anything
else. 'We agree there; love does more harm than
good.'

She knew the competition there would be for a
man with his pulling power so why *was* he choosing her? She said, 'If I'm not drunk I'm punch-
drunk, because to me this doesn't make any sense
at all. I try to pay what I think I owe. You fancy
me and I wouldn't be likely to mistake sex for love,
but that can't be reason enough to make you want
to marry me.'

He reached across the table and took her hand,
and his touch sent a galvanising charge through her,
sending out a storm of conflicting sensations. Nothing like the faint stirrings of desire she had felt for
other men, and she could not have said whether it
was lust or alarm. 'Reason enough,' he said.

She was in no state to argue, and she asked, 'Can
I have some time to think?'

'You can, but time's running out for your
brother-in-law.'

Time had nearly run out for Beth this afternoon.
Max Vella's offer, if he *was* serious, could be the
saving of them. But Sara had to get away from him
now or she could go on jabbering because this had
all the makings of a really monstrous joke.

She asked, 'May I go home?' The food was getting cold on their plates, hardly touched.

'I'll run you back,' he said.

'Thank you.'

When they drew up in the square and he opened the passenger door for her she said, 'Thank you,' again.

'Come to the window and signal all's well,' he said. 'In any case I'll see you tomorrow to hear your answer.'

She was still trying to compose herself as she climbed the stairs. She was not telling Beth nor her mother that Max Vella had asked her to marry him. He was so eligible they would find it as hard to believe as Sara did, but that wouldn't stop them discussing it for hours and she could not face that.

Beth was lying on the sofa in the living room, the door to Sara's bedroom slightly open. 'Where's Mother?' Sara asked.

Beth said, 'I said she could go. Really, Sar, I'm better being quiet. The twins woke up, of course, and I put them in the big bed; they're sound asleep now. How did you get on? Did he offer you a job?'

'Well, yes,' Sara said. She went to her bedroom window and looked down at the lights of the square. Max was still standing on the pavement, beside the car. She opened the window, waved and smiled, signalling no problems, and he raised an acknowledging hand.

'No problems' was a long way from being true, but if there had been trouble waiting for her again she would not have been alone. She could no longer remember a time when she had not been alone, and she was touched that he had shown enough concern to wait and make sure all was well.

'What is the job?' Beth called, and Sara ad-libbed.

'In the library, cataloguing the books. There are hundreds of them.' She had seen the library during her tour of the house and thought it would be a wonderful place for browsing.

'What about the salary?'

'Oh—er—generous.' Whatever was happening, Sara had to keep Beth from cracking up again; she couldn't handle any more histrionics tonight.

And, getting ready for bed, Beth seemed subdued but no longer suicidal. Sara was keeping the pills well away from her. She saw Beth into the bigger bed with the sleeping children and, once in her own bed, toyed with the idea of taking a pill herself. But that would mean getting out of the single bed and going to the kitchen or the bathroom for a glass of water. She couldn't swallow them with her throat dry. Reluctant to move, she stared wide-eyed and wakeful at the walls, wondering what *was* going to happen tomorrow.

When Max Vella came... *If* Max Vella came, because it was easier to believe she had imagined the whole thing than that Vella had actually said, 'I'm asking you to marry me.' If he didn't come, she had imagined it. Or she had drunk too much wine and misheard every word. But she was cold and very sober and she knew that he would come.

When he had seen her reflection in the goldfish

mirror he'd said she'd looked as if she had won the lottery. His proposal was like a lottery win. About the same odds, and from rags to riches. Not that Sara had ever been in rags, although it had sometimes felt like that. The debts had often seemed insurmountable, and now they were. She could never begin to pay off what was owing, and she had thought she had nothing of value left to sell.

A phrase from a Victorian novel she had read years ago came into her mind. A boughten bride. Max Vella was buying himself a bride, like everything else in the Moated House. When he wanted something there was no stopping him, and he had to believe Sara was his for the taking.

Sara's sleep was fitful and troubled until it was almost time to get up when she fell into her first deep slumber, waking to hear Beth pleading, '*Will* you be quiet? Oh, *please* be quiet.'

The twins were active and Beth had a hangover, and Sara, barefoot and wearing a nightshirt, went into the living room. She calmed the twins down, sat Beth at the kitchen table with dry toast, fruit juice and another couple of aspirins, then ran herself a warm, scented bath.

She reckoned Max Vella would arrive here around midday; that gave her about three hours to prepare herself. He had asked her to marry him and she was racked with doubts. Everyone she knew would say she would be mad to refuse him. He was the man who had everything. She had less than nothing, and he was her only hope of saving the ones she loved. He didn't expect her to love him, he was not wanting love. What he was wanting she would find out if she became his wife, and Sara, who had never lacked courage, knew that deep down Max Vella scared her.

She would soak in here until she was relaxed and then she would wash her hair and pick out the best-looking clothes she had and make herself as glamorous as she could. Inside she might be a dithering mess but outside she would be cool. She switched on the radio, finding easy music before she got into the bath. Now she stretched a leg and turned on the hot tap with her toes.

The scent of roses in the bath oil came up in misty clouds, blurring the mirrored tiles on the walls, and she wondered what the aftershave was that Max Vella used. Not one she recognised, but she would know it again anywhere. Very faint. Probably the only understated thing about him. And it was weird that she could almost smell it now through the pungent perfume of roses.

That had to be in her mind. Just as he was. An intruder. In her mind and under her skin. She lay back, letting herself float with the water, some of her tension slipping away as the minutes ticked by. Until the bathroom door opened and Beth shot in, looking panic-stricken, hissing, 'It's him.'

'Who?' Sara jerked up in the bath.

'Max Vella.'

'On the phone?'

'*Here.*'

'Oh, God.' She jumped out of the bath, grabbing

the biggest towel. Would he tell Beth he'd asked
Sara to marry him? What would he tell Beth? Sara
had to keep them apart, and she said, 'Come and
help me find something to wear in the bedroom.'
Then she opened the bathroom door to peer out.

She had to cross the living room. It was a small
room and he was a big man, and although he was
standing well away from her Sara, swathed in her
towel, felt she was brushing up against him as she
sidled along the wall towards her bedroom door.
'Good morning, Sara,' he said.

Inside her bedroom she began to towel herself
dry fast. She had soaked until her skin was a deep
shade of pink, and her hair was a mass of kinking
tendrils. She was a sight, while he was impeccably
groomed and wearing clothes that had cost an arm
and a leg. In every way he always had an unfair
advantage, and she wished she could tell him to go
and come back when she was good and ready. But
if she did she knew he would say, 'No hurry, I'll
wait.' And if Beth heard he had proposed to Sara
it would be Beth's idea of a storybook romance, the
miracle that was going to make everything perfect.

'What did he say?' Sara asked her sister as Beth
went through Sara's wardrobe and Sara pulled undies over her still damp skin.

'That you had business to discuss.'

'Oh, we have.' She dressed hastily and put on a
modicum of eye make-up, lip and cheek gloss and
brushed her hair, wincing as she dragged the brush
through the tangles. Then she went out into the living room where Max Vella was waiting for her,

elegant in brown trousers, brown leather jacket and camel-coloured sweater that had to be cashmere.

He said, 'You take the record. Ten minutes from bath to ready to go.'

She would have liked to take longer. This rush job had done her no favours. She had hardly had time to catch her breath.

When she sat back in his car he asked, 'What was the rush? I didn't flatter myself you were this anxious for my company.'

She might as well admit it. 'I didn't want Beth to hear about last night.'

'That I asked you to marry me? I gathered you hadn't told her when she said she was sure you'd enjoy cataloguing my books. Why didn't you?'

'I didn't tell her because I wasn't sure you meant it.'

'I meant it,' he said.

'Or, if you meant it, what I was going to do. I didn't want pressurising, and Beth might have—'

'Put the pressure on,' he said cynically. 'I'm sure she would. She was ready enough to leave her children with you when she decided to opt out, so why should she balk at letting you marry for money when money is what she needs?'

There was some truth in what he was saying but it was nowhere near the whole truth, and Sara sat sick and silent as the car gathered speed. Marry money? Marry him. What was he rushing her into, this man who had no pity? She turned to face his profile, which looked as hard as if it was chiselled from stone, and said coldly, 'You can have no real idea what you are talking about.'

He turned too, and his smile took most of the harshness from his face. 'That is possible,' he said. 'But I think your little sister has bird bones and a bird brain, and how you two came to be sisters I'll never know.'

His smile was disarming, making what he said seem less scathing, and when he said, 'Forget them all; today it's just you and me,' she said, 'I could do with getting away. Where are we going?'

'Have patience,' he said.

The car was taking her back to the Moated House. Until now it had always seemed like a sparkling fairytale palace to Sara, but as they drove through the gates it almost looked brooding and dark under the heavy skies. At the end of the long drive and over the bridge the car rounded the house, to a helicopter pad alongside a tennis court, and that was when she decided she wouldn't ask any more questions and just let it all happen because it could be one of the most exciting days of her life.

Sara was helped up into the helicopter and strapped into her seat. Max was at the controls, and they rose through a grey mist, the blades spinning above them.

'Last time—the only time—I was in a helicopter,' she said, 'it was a thirty-minute joyride from the local airfield, with everything below spread out like Toytown.'

That day she had been able to recognise landmarks: the river, churches, street patterns, the town square. Cars had seemed smaller than dinky toys, and sheep and cattle had been dots on the green fields. Today she could see nothing below through the dense masses of cloud.

'We're leaving the hills,' Max said. 'Now we're over the town. Your home is down on the left, your office a few inches to the right.'

'If they could see me now.' She had to smile at the thought of friends and colleagues looking up and seeing her flying away with Max Vella. 'Where do we go over next?'

'We cross the racetrack then the motorway.'

'You know just where we are?'

'If I don't we're in big trouble,' he said.

There were those who felt Max Vella *was* big trouble but she wouldn't think about that now. She went on smiling and asked, 'Will you tell me what's down there? Then I can imagine it.'

He summed up their route and very occasionally, when the clouds broke up, she looked down briefly on the scene he was describing before it was blanketed out again. This was not a good day for flying, but Sara was loving it. She might be flying blind but with his hands on the controls she could lean back in her seat and enjoy every minute.

The descent was sudden when it came. 'Here we are,' he said, and they were dropping steadily and smoothly through the clouds. She had glimpsed the sea a few minutes earlier. It stretched now in a grey vista below, with a fringe of shore and a building down there that was either a fair-sized house or a small hotel.

They landed on a lawn as a man and a woman came hurrying across the grass. He was tall and thin with a little goatee beard and hair that the wind was blowing up in wisps, while she was short and plump, in a neat black and white small-check suit and crisp white blouse.

Max hugged the woman, who had gone at him with outflung arms crying, 'How lovely to see you again.'

She smiled at Sara as Max did the introductions. 'Sara, Dot and Harry, two very good friends of mine.' They seemed delighted he was here and Sara wondered if he came often and if he had brought many women who had had to be introduced to Dot and Harry.

'Let's get inside,' Dot was urging; the wind blowing in from the sea was bitterly cold. But once through the front door they were into a foyer, where a log fire burned in a big fireplace and chintz-covered armchairs around made it a cosy, welcoming place. A reception desk showed Sara that it was a hotel.

Dot said, 'I'll be getting back to the kitchen.' And Max went towards an open door beyond which Sara saw a table laid.

She asked, 'Could I freshen up?'

She'd had some idea of making herself more presentable, but when she looked at the face that stared back in the mirror in the little cloakroom she had to admit there wasn't much chance of that. Her hair had dried windblown, her skin was shiny—and all the make-up she had in her handbag was a lipstick and a mascara brush. Added to which she had scrambled into the first outfit Beth had brought out of the cupboard, a jersey two-piece in terracotta and a three-quarter-length black jacket, serviceable enough but nothing special. She should have taken her time this morning instead of panicking. She had better than this in her wardrobe, and the slapdash make-up was hardly a confidence booster.

Maybe when Max took a hard look at her now he'd change his mind about wanting to marry her and she wouldn't be faced with that decision. Then life would go on, getting blacker by the day, because the future would be very dark indeed.

She splashed water on her face, touched up her lipstick and pulled a comb through her hair. In the foyer Dot was bustling out of the room where the table was laid, pushing a trolley with the smile of a cook who knows that her meal is a masterpiece, as the delicious smell of food reached Sara.

Max drew out a chair for her and she seated herself, feasting her eyes on the dishes, a dozen different vegetables, and a beef Wellington with a flaky golden crust and the meat pink and juicy. She could feel her stomach rumbling, her mouth watering, and when Max smiled at her she said, 'If the marriage proposal no longer stands I'm still getting a good meal out of this.'

'It stands,' he said. 'Why shouldn't it stand?'

'I've just looked at myself.'

'You look charming.' She was actually licking her lips. 'And hungry.'

'I'm starving.' She hadn't realised till now when

the sight and the smell of Dot's repast were tickling all her senses. 'I've hardly eaten in two days. What with this and that!'

He said, 'It's high time someone took you in hand.' He put a generous helping of the beef Wellington on her dish, then served up vegetables—a little of everything—and, when she began to protest that was enough he said, 'Two days? It's lucky you didn't slide under the bath water.'

'I had things on my mind.'

'Eat up,' he ordered. He served himself, watching her as she took her first taste of the melting pastry, savouring the flavour and the texture. 'And don't chatter.'

She might have chattered, but every time she started to speak he hushed her so that the meal was eaten in a companionable silence. All the time she was aware of the strength of the quiet man sitting with her and it was reassuring and comforting. Nobody had ever cosseted her before. She ate up and sipped her wine, and didn't say a word until she could manage no more and set down her knife and fork.

'Now we'll talk,' he said.

She drank a little more wine. 'That was delicious. The customers must flock here for Dot's cooking.'

'They do.'

'How many do they have in here now?'

'Only us. They close at the end of October and open again at Easter. I always come down out of season when, officially, the hotel's closed, but Dot and Harry don't mind. I find it's an excellent bolt-hole.'

'Bolt-hole?' she echoed.

'You know what a bolt-hole is?'

'Of course I do. Somewhere where no one can get at you.'

'Unless you want them to. I usually stay five or six days.' He topped up her glass and then his own. 'That brings us to next weekend. I could get you back to your sister this evening, or if you stay on here with me I'll give you a thousand pounds a day.'

CHAPTER FOUR

SARA choked on her wine and Max said, 'We're talking days here, not nights. Separate rooms.'

That would be easier, but she didn't like the idea of being offered cash for her company and she said, her expression showing her distaste, 'You'd pay me to stay?'

'Look on it as a small investment on my part.' What exactly did he mean by that?

She said, 'Anyhow I couldn't just stay on. There's home, there's the office.'

'Ring your sister and tell her you're travelling around collecting antiquarian books for this library you're supposed to be cataloguing.'

'She'd never believe that.'

'She's gullible enough to believe anything,' Max drawled. 'Especially if the money's good.'

He despised Beth's weakness, but Sara bit back a hot retort and said coldly, 'And what tale do you suggest I should be telling them at work?'

'You've got a week's leave of absence there.'

That choked her so that she croaked, 'You fixed that? Who with?'

'John Mellors and Jim Kelly.' The owner of the *Chronicle* and the editor.

'You said I'd be away for a week with you?'

'Yes.' Max Vella had told them he was bringing

72

her down here, she was staying down here, and they had said fair enough because he was Max Vella. She had to hold down a surge of rage that left her seething. He was so sure Sara must do what he planned for her that it was a struggle to keep her voice below screaming pitch. 'You take too much for granted, Mr Vella, because I would prefer to go home, thank you very much. The money is good and I'm sure the food would be fantastic—' she was into heavy sarcasm now '—but I really do dislike the idea of you fixing where I shall be and what I should be doing as if I were your property with no choice or say in the matter.'

'Of course you have options.' His deep, slow voice was emphasising her shrillness. 'You can stay or go. I can take too much for granted, that's one of my bad habits, but if we spend a few days here together you'll have the opportunity of checking my other habits before deciding whether you can face a lifetime with me.

'If you find you can't, you still have the choice to walk away. And although a few thousand wouldn't go far towards settling your family debts they could be better than nothing.'

Her anger was ebbing as she listened. He was offering her a chance to get to know him better before she committed herself for what could be the rest of her life and she could hardly object to that. Nor could she afford to turn down his thousand-a-day offer when they needed the money so desperately.

She asked, 'And will you be looking out for my bad habits?'

He smiled that smile that made her reluctantly smile too. 'I know what I'm getting; you're the one who's holding back.'

She protested, 'I don't even have a toothbrush.'

'I'm sure the hotel can provide one. Tomorrow we'll get what you need.'

At a thousand a day she could buy herself essentials. She said wryly, 'All I've brought is a lipstick, a pack of tissues and that box of sleeping pills.' She must phone Beth, make sure that she would be safe for a few days.

Max said, 'I assure you we will be in separate rooms; there'll be no need to dope my coffee.'

And suddenly she was joking, 'It wouldn't work, would it? Somehow you'd see me. Somehow I'd be the idiot to take them.'

She did resent him arranging this without consulting her but that was the way of tycoons, and she was realising that she wanted to stay. She could hardly remember her last break from routine, and Max Vella would surely be a fantastic companion. She said, 'I'll phone Beth, but she isn't going to believe I'm hunting down old books.'

'Care to bet on that?' he said.

It was as well she didn't because Beth did accept it. Sara rang her from a small kiosk in the foyer and Beth said she was sure Sara would find some wonderful bargains. They were staying with friends of Max Vella's, Sara told her, and Beth thought that sounded nice. She did say, 'He's a big noise, isn't he? But you know how to look after yourself, don't you?'

'Oh, every time,' Sara said. 'Where can I ring you tomorrow?'

Beth thought she'd stay on at Sara's flat until Sara came back—she said she was so sorry she'd behaved the way she had. She was sure now that things were going to get better.

'She believed it,' Sara said to Max when she returned to find him standing by the fireplace. And it did sound less unlikely than that Sara was staying down here to make up her mind whether she was going to be a rich man's wife or let Jeremy go to jail.

'Shall we go for a walk on the beach?' Max said. He was wearing an overcoat and he carried a woman's quilted coat that swaddled Sara.

Outside darkness had come down. Sara could taste the salt in the air and hear the sea but there were no stars, no moonlight, and when Max took her hand she blinked and peered and gasped, 'I can't see a thing.'

'The path's easy most of the way down,' he said. 'By the time we reach the rocks your eyes will be accustomed.' It would not have surprised her if he could see in the dark like a jungle cat, and she would rather have waited till she could see for herself. But he was right, the path was gradual, and the pitch-blackness was lightening. When they reached the shingle she could make out the shape of the rocks and see the cliffs rearing up around the cove.

Down here the sounds of the sea and the wind mingled like wild music as the waves came crashing in. They walked with his arm around her at the sea's edge, her hair blowing all ways. By daylight this could be a pleasant coastal scene, but darkness made it strange. It would take a hurricane to blow Max off his feet but gusts of wind were slamming into Sara, and when she lurched against him he said, 'You could do with a bit more ballast.'

'You think I need fattening up?'

'You will if you often go for days without food.'

'I don't.'

'I'm glad to hear it, but what I am saying is that you'd better hang onto me.'

His face above hers was dark, the white scar cutting through the heavy eyebrow. His mouth was closing on hers, and she closed her eyes because she couldn't be sure how she would react when he kissed her. He said, 'You're shivering.' And he was not kissing her. 'We'll go back,' he said.

If she was shaking inside the thick coat it was because the wind was so cold, and because she was relieved that he had not kissed her—she wanted the separate rooms, and even one deep kiss might have taken her into his bed tonight.

Her room was delightful—sprigged wallpaper, curtains and bedcover, Victorian furnishings, but as comfortable as a cherished home. Dot had greeted them in the foyer to ask if there was anything else they needed. Max had ordered coffee and brandy, and when Sara had said no thanks he had said, 'I'll see you in the morning. Sleep well.'

Dot had brought Sara up to her room. There were toiletries, including a toothbrush, in the little bathroom. There was also a new nightgown laid out on the bed with a high neck and long sleeves in flannelette. One of Dot's, Sara guessed. She washed her hair and sat cross-legged in front of an electric fire, drying and brushing it, and wondered what she would do if Max knocked on the door. She thought he would smile at the sight of her in Dot's nightgown but tonight he had said he would see her tomorrow, and if he had planned on rushing her he would surely have kissed her on the beach.

She had so much on her mind that she should have lain awake half the night but almost as soon as her head touched the pillow she was gone, and if she had any dreams they did not disturb her.

The next time she opened her eyes it was daylight, and Max was standing fully dressed beside the bed.

She sat up, pulling the quilt up to her chin. 'How long have you been here?'

'A few minutes. Breakfast's ready. Then we'll go shopping.'

She had just over ten pounds in her purse and a small agreed overdraft in her bank account. She said, 'I don't know about that.'

'The nightdress is a knockout.' He grinned, because the nightdress was sensible and warm and that was all it was. 'And I'm sure Dot could lend you more from her wardrobe.'

Dot's style was not Sara's, neither was her shape, and Sara grinned too. 'Please let's go shopping,' she said.

There was a car waiting beside the hotel, and before they drove away Max handed her a wad of notes, high and low denominations. 'Expenses,' he said. 'Let me know if you need more.'

She wished she could have managed these next few days without him subbing her. She would take the thousand a day but she would have liked a small show of independence, although she was here with only the outfit she stood up in because he had given her no warning.

It would have been lovely to go for real luxury cosmetics and clothes, but she stayed with the economy make-up she usually used and she bought some undies, a couple of dresses, a pair of walking shoes, a pair of jeans and a sweater, none of which was exorbitantly priced.

Max usually waited outside shops for her and Sara smiled at seeing how women's heads swivelled when they saw him standing there, not because they knew who he was but because he was such a stunningly sexy man.

In one shop window there was a cashmere trench coat. Max said, 'That would suit you.'

She said, 'Very classy,' and came out with the sweater.

'Where's the coat?'

'I've got a coat, I don't need to buy another coat.'

'Humour me,' he said.

It fitted as if it had been made for her, and she

told herself that it was no more to him than buying ice-cream treats for the twins would be to her. She still had the option of saying no to marrying him. She could hand the coat back if she refused him. But when he turned up the collar of the coat so that it framed her face she felt as if he was wrapping her up, soft and warm, keeping her safe.

This was the first real holiday Sara had had in years, and she was laughing more than she had in years. Max could have her giggling helplessly. His off-beat humour hit her funny bone every time, and she always seemed able to make him smile. She saw the effect of his authority wherever they went—Max Vella was always given the best table in restaurants and got immediate attention in stores.

Sara was enjoying herself immensely. Whether they ate alone in the little dining room sharing Dot's meals, or in other hotels, cafés and pubs, the food always tasted good. Everything seemed good. Every day was bright and clear and sharp even when it rained and the winds were cold. They walked for miles along the coastline, and explored cobble-stoned villages and ruined castles.

Thursday afternoon, looking for gifts for Sara to take back for the twins, they found a magical shop full of toys fashioned by craftsmen: traditional rocking horses, farms, forts and castles, waddling animals and music makers. Sara was looking for something cheerful and found two hobbyhorses, one with a dappled grey head, one silky black.

The black one brought back a wistful memory. 'I had a black horse,' she told Max. 'In the old days when I rode over the hills and looked down on the Moated House I was riding Black Bess. I named her after Dick Turpin the highwayman's horse.' Bess had gone with everything else when Sara's father had died and the hard times had started.

Max smiled at her. 'I can imagine how you looked,' he said. 'On your black horse with your red hair flying.'

She still could not visualise him at fourteen, when he had first seen the Moated House. He had been big for his age and must have been handsome, but his face now was too worldly, too experienced; all signs of the boy had gone.

In the toy shop Sara felt she was acting like a child and Max was spoiling her like a child, which was pleasant enough, but she was a woman and she had begun to wonder why he was making no move to seduce her. There was opportunity, and the sexual rapport was strong. Instinctively she knew he would be a superb lover. Every time he touched her or smiled at her it was almost as though he had pulled her against him. Almost but not quite.

That night they ate at the small hotel and then went down to the beach again. There was a near-gale blowing. Sea spray filled the air so that they came back windblown, and Sara was still breathless when they reached the top of the stairs and Max asked, 'Will you stay in my room tonight?'

The days she had spent with Max had made her more physically aware of him by the hour. During the nights in her separate bed she had thought about him, dreamt about him as a lover more than once.

She wanted him, and she might have said, Yes, please, yes, I will, there's nowhere I'd rather be, but somehow she was still too breathless to get out more than 'Yes.' And they passed her door and he opened the door to his room.

She had not been in here before. It was less fussy than her room and bigger. The bed was much bigger too, and she wondered how many other women had slithered between those sheets. Since he had made his millions, all Max Vella's women would be stars but even while he had been fighting to the top he must have always had the sensual charisma that would have got him desirable, experienced partners. He found Sara desirable. Beautiful and desirable, he had told her, but now it came to naked surrender she could be a let-down for a man who had seen it all and knew it all.

Max's dark springy hair didn't seem wet at all, but Sara's hair was cold and clammy on her shoulders and her little black dress seemed to be sticking to her. She hugged herself for warmth and with every step he took towards her she could feel her bones getting weaker so that when he reached her she was leaning against the wall for support. Her arms were folded tightly across her breasts, her fingers dug into the soft flesh of her upper arms, and she croaked, 'I hope you're not expecting too much because I haven't been around that much, I—'

'For God's sake stop gabbering,' he said. He cupped her face in his hands and kissed her gently, taking her quivering lips slowly until they parted and his kisses became deeper. Before she'd met this man her mind had always kept a check on her body, but nothing had prepared her for the sweet urgency of these kisses. She found herself reciprocating, standing on tiptoe, her hands clasped behind his head as he held her against him.

As he undressed her she closed her eyes and it took no time at all. When he carried her to the bed she watched him get undressed. The deep-tanned skin and the rippling muscles made him look as hard and as splendid as a bronze statue, but when he lay down beside her and drew her close he was warm as she moved into his arms.

This was right. In this they were good together. His hand cupped a breast and her fingers found the sinews at his shoulder blades, and the shivers that were rippling through her now were like the waves on the shore. But suddenly, with no further warning, in an explosion of passion she was all feeling and beyond reason, as though the sea had her and was caressing and arousing every nerve, making her blood sing and driving her in a mounting crescendo until she was riding the storm that was riding her.

When the tidal wave came she went soaring with it, and the man who was part of her. It was such mind-blowing ecstasy, she could have gone on screaming for joy but then she heard the thudding of her own heart and came down into the real world. Max lay beside her. 'I told you we were right for each other,' he said, and he lifted a hand to his lips.

She could have been washed onto the beach from a stormy sea, she was that exhausted, but her spine was still getting frissons from his touch, and she wondered, How much practice does it take to make a man into a demon lover? She was the one who had gone out of her mind while Max had been in control; she was almost sure of that. She wasn't complaining, it had been wonderful, and she said, 'You did bring me down here to seduce me.'

'No,' he said. 'I brought you here to marry you.'

'You're joking.' She had said that before when he'd asked her to marry him. Again, he said, 'No.'

'But we can't. I mean, just like that you can't.'

'We have a marriage licence, and the hotel's licensed for weddings. If we go back married I can shield you from most of the publicity and the gossip. I'd take care of you, which would obviously include settling your family debts.'

'When would it be?'

'Two o'clock tomorrow afternoon.'

That meant that this time tomorrow she could be his wife, and if she tried to argue while she was lying naked in his arms he could probably seduce her into agreeing. There was no question of being in love, but his love making had aroused a sensual hunger in her that could make her vulnerable. She said, 'It's too sudden...'

'Hush,' he said, and drew her gently against the strong length of his body. 'Go to sleep.'

I'll never sleep, she thought. This can't be happening. Tomorrow morning we must talk about this, calmly and sensibly. But as she lay still the weariness came back until her limbs slackened and her

eyelids closed and she drifted into the dream-
less dark.

She woke next morning to find Max, dressed,
holding a cup of tea, and her first thought was how
incredible this was—Max Vella bringing in the
morning tea. Then she remembered last night.

She sat upright squeaking, 'Did you say we were
getting married this afternoon?'

'A *fait accompli* would cut out a lot of the fuss.'
He put the cup on the table beside the bed. 'Unless
you're wanting a big wedding.'

'*No!*' Emphatically not. Sara had never dreamt
of a white wedding with all the trappings, and in
their case it would be hypocrisy. She said, 'I'd
much prefer a quiet civil ceremony.'

'Then that's settled.'

She couldn't dither any longer. She wanted to
protest but maybe it was for the best. She had to
marry him. If she didn't it would be like handing
Beth the pills again, and last night had shown how
potent the chemistry was between them. She liked
him, she admired him. She would be crazy not to
marry him, although she still couldn't understand
why he wanted to marry her.

'Drink your tea,' he said.

Just twenty minutes later she was ready to go
downstairs and face Harry and Dot. They would be
her first experience of how Max Vella's friends
would react when he produced a wife most of them
had never heard of before. But Harry smiled at her,
saying, 'Congratulations are in order, then?' And
Dot, piping a delicate white tracery around a white-

iced bridal cake, was beaming as if a wedding at the shortest of notices was just what she needed to brighten her day.

After breakfast, Sara and Max walked along the coast again, this morning climbing the cliffs in a blustery wind that made the going rough. She was glad of that. A gentle stroll might have given her time to start wondering what the future held. Her qualms could have turned into a full-blown panic attack if she had stopped to do some serious thinking. But scrambling around on cliffs, even with Max holding her hand, was strenuous enough to need her full attention, until it was one o'clock and they were walking back again through the front door of the little hotel.

'Dot will come up to help you change,' Max said.

'I don't need anyone. I can get into something fairly suitable.'

'You might have second thoughts on your own. Now Dot's iced the cake there's no way out.' He was joking, but there *was* no way out. If Sara tried to run, where could she run to? And Dot, wearing a lilac velvet jacket over a cream-coloured dress, was with her before Sara had got beyond the stage of opening her wardrobe door and staring at the clothes that were hanging there.

She had never realised she might be shopping for her wedding but she had bought a calf-length chiffon dress, a floral print of white marguerites on a blue background, and Dot said, 'Oh, I like that, and there's something blue in it.' She quoted gaily,

'Something old, something new, something borrowed, something blue.'

Dot fussing around was better than Sara preparing for her secret wedding all alone. Dot made her smile, telling her about her own wedding day over thirty years ago when Harry and his brother had popped into the pub opposite for several quick ones, got the time wrong and rushed down the aisle for the wedding booked before theirs. Just as the vicar asked if anyone knew of any impediment why the marriage should not take place.

'And when our guests started to arrive there were still some of the other guests waiting to warn me I could be marrying a lunatic.' Whether any of this was true or not it made Sara laugh.

Dot helped with her hair, producing a tortoiseshell Spanish comb—something borrowed—and fixing tiny white silk flowers in Sara's bright tresses.

'You look beautiful,' Dot said encouragingly. 'A really bonny bride.'

Sara didn't feel bonny. She hardly recognised her own reflection. Her eyes seemed wider and darker than she had ever seen them, and under the makeup her skin was pale enough to have Dot, who had arrived with a bottle of brandy, pouring out a stiff measure. 'Get it down,' Dot urged. 'Can't have you going down with stage fright.'

'Or having second thoughts.'

And Dot chuckled, 'No danger of that with Max waiting for you. Come on, now.'

Sara gulped and the raw spirit burned her throat

but it didn't warm her as she would have expected. She still felt chilled to the bone.

'Five minutes to two,' Dot said. 'They'll be ready for us.' She did a quick check of her own reflection, patting her silver curls. 'Here we go,' she said.

The door of the lounge was open to the entrance hall. No music was playing 'Here Comes the Bride' and there were no friends or family. Just Dot, trotting beside Sara, and down there Max Vella waiting for Sara to make him a lifetime's commitment.

She walked steadily, keeping her head up, getting down the staircase and then crossing the hall to the open door. A pleasant room. Spacious and light, chairs, settees, small tables around, and a bower of flowers at the far end. Max, Harry and a woman waited, and the room blurred at the edge of Sara's vision.

The brandy had to be making everything hazy. Harry and the woman closed in on her as she reached them, but Max was the only one who seemed solid, and when Sara stood beside him everyone else was shadowy.

The registrar was reading the words of contract. 'Repeat after me. I call upon these persons here present to witness that I, Max Vella, take thee, Sara Solway, to be my lawful wedded wife.'

Max said the words in his usual drawling voice, deep with no hurry and no hesitation, and then it was Sara's turn.

The registrar was smiling at her. She had a cute face, a button nose and rather large teeth. 'I call upon these persons…' said the registrar.

Max was wearing a superbly cut dark suit. He looked such a powerful man with hooded eyes and his mouth in a hard, straight line, waiting for Sara to speak. After the intimacy of the last few days he seemed a stranger again, and seconds dragged by as she swallowed, her tongue flicking between dry lips.

But she had agreed to marry him and nobody went back on a bargain struck with Max Vella. 'I call upon these persons here present…', she began, and it was almost over.

Max put a ring on her finger, the register was signed, witnessed by Dot and Harry, and it was over. Max had bought her, she was his boughten bride. She grabbed a chair and sat down, and Max asked her, 'Are you all right?'

'Never better,' she said quickly.

Wedding nerves, said the registrar's smile, and Dot and Harry went with the registrar to her car in the car park. Sara twisted the ring on her finger and asked in the same bright voice, 'How did you know my size for the ring?'

'A lucky guess,' he said.

A fraction large, because she could turn it around. Her head was swimming and she pushed her hair back. The Spanish comb slid out, the tiny flowers tumbling into her lap.

She babbled, 'Now I look like Medusa. I must fix my hair; could I go and fix my hair?'

They went through the empty hall upstairs to Sara's room and she sat at the dressing table, watching Max begin to pour brandy into the glass. 'If that's for me,' she said, 'I don't need another. Dot gave me some for stage fright and it seems to have gone to my head. I don't often get the vapours.'

There was another good old Victorian word. Boughten brides always got the vapours.

'It was those bloody flowers,' he said. 'Dot must have emptied the flower shop.'

It was not the flowers nor the brandy. It was being scared of the thought that even now she might just have made a terrible mistake. But Max was smiling and Sara tried to smile too. She said, 'The flowers were lovely. Dot made the room look lovely. She certainly knows the rules for these affairs.' And she quoted, 'Something old, something new, something borrowed, something blue.'

He looked blank. 'What rules are they?'

'You haven't heard of them?'

'No.'

'Well everybody else has; it's what a bride's supposed to have.'

'Something old—I should qualify there.'

He was keeping her smiling and she said, 'You're not that much older than me.'

'My dear girl,' he said, 'I'm at least six lifetimes older than you.'

'Never mind, you're wearing well,' she joked. Now that the contract was signed she had to believe there was no reason why this should not work. It could. It must. And she would not let herself admit that she could just have been railroaded into marriage by a man who had had lifetimes of experience at taking what he wanted.

CHAPTER FIVE

THEY left the hotel after lunch on Sunday, going out to the helicopter that had stood on the lawn all week. Dot and Harry were there to say goodbye. Harry shook Max's hand. 'Safe journey,' said Harry. 'Thank you for everything.'

'Thank you,' Max said.

Dot hugged Sara and told her, 'It's been lovely having you here.' Her face puckered anxiously and she sighed. 'I do hope you'll be happy.'

She's sorry for me, Sara thought. I'm married to a fabulously wealthy man whom they both admire so why is she sorry for me?

Through a break in the dark clouds, as the helicopter rose, Sara looked down at the small hotel on the cliffs, and the two tiny figures, and wished she could have stayed with them longer, but the holiday—the honeymoon of sorts—was over. She was flying away into unknown territory with a man who was still a mystery to her. She didn't know much more about him than she had when she had tried to interview him.

Physically, yes, but in every other way there were limits to their closeness. When she looked at him now he didn't turn his head. He must have no end of crises and decisions waiting for him after the week's break he had just taken, and she felt he was so preoccupied he had almost forgotten he had a passenger, that if she put a hand on his arm it would startle him.

He was shutting her out, and she had problems enough of her own to ponder through an almost silent journey, although she did learn one more thing about him before they landed. They hit turbulence and the little vehicle dropped, as if stepping into a lift shaft without a lift. Sara shrieked, her vivid imagination having them plummeting to the ground.

It couldn't have been more than seconds before they were on a fairly even keel again but she was still nervous; the helicopter had suddenly seemed very small and fragile. She gasped, 'Are we going to be all right?'

'Of course.' He must have come across air pockets countless times but this was new to her.

She grimaced. 'I'm the one who always screams the loudest on fairground rides.'

She got a slight smile at that, and she wondered, how long it had been since he had screamed. She said, 'You don't panic, do you?'

'Only as a last resort.'

She wanted to ask him when he had last been scared witless, but she knew that he would be no more likely to panic than he would be to fall in love. Ice-cool and in control whatever happened. Maybe there was nothing that would intimidate him, and she found this insight into his character rather daunting.

She spent the last half-hour of the journey trying

to psych herself into looking and sounding at ease because when she walked into the manor house with its master she would need all the dignity she could muster. Most of them in there would remember her as the redhead from the *Chronicle* who had been carrying on shamelessly with Max Vella last weekend in front of half the county.

As she was helped down from the helicopter she wondered if the men in green overalls knew she was Vella's wife, or if to them she was just another girl who had taken off with the boss for a few steamy days and nights and was now being returned to base.

The woman who had the door open for them was a Mrs Thomson, the housekeeper. Sara knew her by sight. Now she gave Sara a frosty smile and beamed all her attention to Max, telling him, 'Mr Druitt is here, sir.'

'I'll have a word with him,' said Max. He had taken a few steps before he noticed that Sara was standing, not knowing whether she was supposed to follow or not, and he almost snapped his fingers at her. 'Come along.'

I could be a puppy dog, she thought resentfully. He's spent enough time on me these last few days. Now I'm expected to trot to his orders... She was several paces behind him when he opened a door and went into a room, and a man said heartily, 'Hello, good to see you. I've brought the papers you wanted.'

'First of all,' said Max, 'I'd like you to meet my wife.'

'Well this is a surprise.' The man sounded as if he was smiling. 'Well perhaps not all that surprising.' Max drew Sara forward and a dapper little man, in a grey suit, shirt and tie, got a surprise that wiped the smile off his face and made his eyes bulge because it was clear that Sara was not the one he had expected to see.

He recovered quickly but he still looked pole-axed. 'How do you do? I'm delighted to meet you,' he said, when Sara knew he was wondering, Where did you come from, and who the heck are you?

Max said, 'Mrs Thomson will show you to our room; I'll be right with you.' And Sara turned to see the housekeeper, standing behind her, rigid with shock.

'This way,' said Mrs Thomson after gulping twice, and she went off down the hall with Sara following. 'When did this happen?' she asked, staring straight ahead.

'On Friday,' said Sara.

'You married Mr Vella this Friday?'

'That's right.'

'Oh!' said Mrs Thomson, seemingly at a loss for words. She led the way upstairs and opened a door, showing Sara into a big room with a king-sized bed, panelled walls and antique furniture. 'I'll send your cases up,' she said, 'and get them unpacked for you.' And beat a fast retreat, obviously hotfooting it to tell the rest of the staff all about their new mistress who was a most unsuitable lady of the manor.

The house would soon be buzzing with the news

and in no time at all so would half the town. Sara should be phoning Beth and her mother. There was a phone on a writing desk by the window, and as Sara walked across to it Max came into the room. 'All right?' he asked.

'More or less. I did say once before that I felt like Medusa. Well I think I must be her because I can turn everyone to stone.'

'Only briefly.' He smiled and she pulled a face.

'But how long before they come out of it? I left Mr Druitt about to keel over and Mrs Thomson as stiff as a poker.' Max laughed at that. 'May I phone Beth?' she asked.

'If you must.'

The last time Sara had spoken to her sister had been on Thursday. She hadn't known then that she would be getting married on Friday, but she had told Beth that she would be back on Sunday and they would see what could be done, and Beth had promised she wouldn't do anything silly in the meantime.

Now Sara tapped the digits and listened to the ringing of her own phone in her little flat, wondering how to break the news. 'Yes?' said someone in a hoarse whisper.

'Beth?' asked Sara, and Beth screeched.

'Sar? Oh, thank God. Oh, Sar, I've been praying you'd phone. They're after Jeremy. They came to the house after him. He got out the back way and he came here, but they're sure to come here and—'

'Where is he now?' Sara managed to get in.

'*Here*, in your flat. You know what they said they

were going to do to him. They're really going to hurt him. Oh, Sar, where can we go?'

'Tell them to come here,' said Max. He might not have caught every word but Beth's shrieks had reached him.

'Max says come to the Moated House,' said Sara.

'Is that where you are?'

'Yes.'

'We'll all be right with you,' Beth whimpered.

Sara put down the phone and looked up at Max. 'The heavies have lost patience,' she said. 'Jeremy's just ahead of the ones who've been threatening to break his legs.'

Max's expression worried her, grim as a hanging judge, as if no pleading would get through to him. She said, 'I know what you're thinking.'

'That it hasn't taken long for the vultures to gather,' he said cynically.

Beth was no vulture, just a frightened girl frantic for her man. Sara said, 'You promised to help.' And hated having to remind him. She added bitterly, 'Should I have got it in writing?'

'You got my word,' he said curtly, and she should have known that would be enough. 'Douglas Druitt's a lawyer; that's why he's here. Tomorrow he would have been meeting your family. I would have preferred them to have held off till then, but it'll have to be today instead. I'll warn Douglas. When they arrive bring them into the library.'

She murmured, 'Thank you.' And he raised the scarred eyebrow.

'Why thank me? This was part of the bargain.'

It had been, of course, but a flush burned on her cheekbones and she ducked her head to hide it from him. He had bought her and he was paying, and making her feel she would be earning every penny.

She followed him out of the bedroom and went into a room with windows overlooking the forecourt, the bridge, and the long drive where she should get a first glimpse of anything turning in through the open gates from the road.

Jeremy's car was a white Fiesta which would be easy to spot, but if his creditors had been banging on the front door while he'd been escaping through the back he could have bolted on foot. In that case they might be in Sara's car.

The first car she saw was a yellow taxi and she hurried down the great staircase, across the hall to the front door, running down the wide steps outside into a bitter little wind as the taxi came over the bridge. As soon as it stopped Beth and the twins spilled out. Beth gathered up Josh and grabbed Joanne's hand, racing with them both towards Sara. She looked as distraught as a refugee from a war zone, dropping Josh to fling herself into Sara's arms. Both twins clung to their mother's skirt, although Joanne peeked up at Sara to whisper, 'Did you bring us some pressies?'

'I did,' said Sara. 'You shall have them tomorrow.' And she asked Beth, 'Anybody after you?'

Beth was shivering from fear rather than cold. 'No, but they would have been. They were coming for him; I'm sure the taxi passed their car. They couldn't have seen us, but—'

'You'll be all right now,' Sara reassured her. 'Max is waiting with his lawyer, but before we go in I've got something to tell you. I'm married. I married Max Vella while we were away.'

Beth swayed as if someone had hit her, croaking, 'You didn't. You couldn't have. It can't be legal.'

'Believe it,' said Sara, which was too much for Beth. She was making little mewing sounds of disbelief but Jeremy chortled.

'But this is *fantastic*.' His fair hair had tumbled over his forehead and there was a sheen of sweat there and on his upper lip, but now he was smiling a wide, merry grin. 'Hey, when Beth told me you'd gone away with Max Vella I thought maybe he'd be good for a loan if you played your cards right. But you *married* him. He's family now; how did you manage that, you clever little sister?'

'You don't know much about Max if you think you can con him,' Sara said coldly, and that stopped Jeremy grinning.

'God, no, I wouldn't try that,' he was protesting all the way into the house. Beth was stunned, looking about her in an unfocused fashion.

In the hall Max waited without moving a muscle, and his stillness seemed more dangerous to Sara than any show of strength. Mrs Thomson was there, and Max said, 'Take care of the children, will you?'

She was not a complete battleaxe. The twins, especially now they were a picture of wide-eyed innocence, were beautiful, and Mrs Thomson said, 'I have some very special cookies in the kitchen.'

That's more than she'd offer me, thought Sara as they trotted off with the smiling housekeeper.

'Come this way,' said Max, 'and we'll get down to business.' He went ahead, leading them out of the hall, along a wide passageway where there were paintings on the wall, pieces of furniture, all costly, covetable stuff. Jeremy, walking behind Max, was darting quick glances around, probably, Sara thought savagely, revelling in the prospect that as Max Vella's wife Sara would be a golden touch.

Much he knew about it. Max wouldn't be bailing Beth's husband out twice, and Sara had never felt angrier with Jeremy. Beth was staring around too, as if she couldn't believe her eyes nor her ears and this was some crazy dream. More than once she almost stumbled, and when Sara put a hand on her arm she stared at the gold band on Sara's finger as if it hypnotised her.

Jeremy had been walking quite jauntily, but when Max opened the library door and turned to face him he seemed to shrink and cringe. Douglas Druitt stood up from a seat at a table near the window, and Max pointed to a chair facing Druitt. 'Sit down,' he said to Jeremy.

Against a wall just inside the room was a carved wooden settle. Sara sat on that, drawing Beth down beside her. The action would be at the other end of the room, between the men at the table where Jeremy and the lawyer sat and Max Vella loomed over them.

'We have the figures.' The lawyer pushed sheets of paper across the table.

Jeremy glanced at them, gasped, then blustered, 'How did you get this? Most of this should be confidential.'

'Don't waste my time,' Vella drawled, and after that Jeremy was silent, turning one page after another.

'Well?' said Druitt, and Jeremy nodded, slowly and heavily.

Beth was so white-faced that Sara thought she was fainting and put an arm around her. Her voice was so low Sara had to watch her lips to read the words, 'What is he going to do?'

She didn't mean Jeremy. Max Vella was the man in charge. 'I don't know,' Sara said, and the lawyer spoke for Vella when Jeremy sagged back in his chair and looked up helplessly.

'Your creditors will be contacted and your debts will be transferred.' Jeremy began to babble thanks as Druitt went on, 'You will pay back on agreed terms. You understand?' Jeremy was nodding. 'You will owe Mr Vella, and Mr Vella does not have bad debts.'

So Max had told Sara. She had believed him, and so did Jeremy, who was still nodding as the lawyer picked up a mobile phone. Druitt made several calls. It was late Sunday afternoon with offices closed so he had to be contacting private numbers. But as soon as he mentioned Max Vella he got through to the names he asked for, and there followed brief conversations when he gave Vella as guarantor.

Putting down the phone, he said, 'Well that should hold off the hounds.'

'I can't tell you how grateful I am,' said Jeremy.

'Don't try,' said Vella. 'Don't give me any trouble, and never consider making a run for it. Because there is no hiding place where one day soon you wouldn't come face to face with me or those who are acting for me. And on that day you'd wish you had let the thugs you were running from break your legs.'

Beside Sara, Beth moaned very softly, and Sara thought, No hiding place for Jeremy or for me. We are both Max's prisoners.

'However,' said Max. 'We can come to an easy arrangement. I'll give you a job and I'll settle for half the amount owed, with repayments that should leave you a comfortable lifestyle.'

'God, yes,' said Jeremy eagerly.

'On condition,' said Max, 'that you and your wife keep away from my wife. And there is no further contact with her from either of you.'

'What?' Beth sounded strangled. She grabbed Sara's arm and was holding on tight while Sara was dumbstruck. If she started speaking she could end up howling, You can't do this unless you want one of the shortest marriages on record. When my sister and her children leave I am out of here... But that kind of outburst would only sound hysterical, and she struggled to slow her racing heart and collect her wits.

Max was saying, 'You might like to consider

this. It will be safe to go home; there's a car waiting. Go to your own house not Sara's flat.'

The lawyer stood up and Jeremy got out of his chair and came towards the door where Beth and Sara stood. When he reached them he took Beth's hand and put a trembling hand on Sara's arm. His voice shook; probably for the first time he was genuinely shocked by what he had brought on Beth and Sara. 'Take care, Sar,' he said hoarsely. 'We know what you've always done for us, what you're doing for us now.' Then Max Vella's shadow fell across them and Jeremy's hand fell from Sara's arm as if Vella had struck it away.

Druitt was holding the door open for Jeremy and Beth. Beth was in tears and Jeremy looked back helplessly at Sara as they went. 'Don't forget to collect the children,' she called out after them. Then she turned to face Max, her voice as cold and clear as chipped ice. 'Well I can see why you wouldn't want your life cluttered up with the likes of them, but did you always intend breaking us up? Keeping my family away from me?'

'Why not?' he drawled. 'Bolton's a born shyster, your sister's a born victim.'

'You think I don't know that?' She was forcing the words through clenched teeth. 'And they're the second generation. My father was a conman, my mother's so gullible she lives in cloud-cuckoo-land. How do you think the twins will turn out? I reckon Josh could be the pushover and Joanne could be the one with a sharp eye for the main chance.'

She was trying to talk through her fury, jabbering

to fill an angry silence, but it wasn't helping, she was still flaming, and she ended with, 'And this wasn't one of the conditions we agreed on.

'No, this was one of my very rare impulses, a spur of the moment decision. When I met Bolton and saw your sister clinging to you like a leech I thought a codicil to my financial offer might be amusing.'

'*Amusing?*' She spat that out.

'And instructive. Showing how much value they put on all you've done for them over the years. We've named a price.'

'That's blackmail.'

'They're the blackmailers. You've always been the dupe. I am offering them a final settlement.'

'Beth won't wear it.' But it would be an agonising choice for Beth—the sister, whose support she needed, or the man she loved.

'Care to bet on it?' he drawled, and she wanted to smash something precious and valuable belonging to him. Like knocking over the antique globe of the world and jumping on it, but if she tried that he would grab her and she did not want him touching her.

She said coldly, 'I'd like to freshen up; I'm sticky after the journey.'

'Of course. By the way Douglas will be with us for dinner; he's staying overnight.'

That halted her in the doorway. 'I'll certainly look forward to dinner with Douglas,' she said. 'He must really be wondering where you found me, coming from such a nice family. I wasn't the one he expected, was I, when you said "meet my wife"? Whoever she was, Douglas must be thinking you made a rotten choice.'

A red mist of rage was still in front of her eyes. As she said that she blinked it away and saw Max's face, and what she saw made her get out of the room and walk away quickly. She had gone too far with that remark. She had seen that in the tightening of his jaw muscles, but she got no triumph from having scored a hit.

Sara found her way back to the bedroom with no trouble at all, walking through the great house of which she was mistress in name only. At first there was no sign of her belongings, but she found her clothes hanging in a closet in a dressing room leading off the bedroom, undies in a drawer.

She was dreading the hours ahead sitting at dinner with Max, who was probably as angry with her as she was with him, and the lawyer who had just witnessed a scene of such scalding humiliation to her. What kind of small talk could there be? About the weather? The food? Druitt might ask what she had done for a living, where she had lived. He might ask nothing personal at all after meeting Jeremy and Beth and seeing Max order them out of the house, but his beady eyes would be sure to be running over Sara.

She had never felt so lonely in her life. For all their faults her mother and her sister loved her as dearly as she loved them, but Max would never understand that. Love couldn't touch him, and he made no allowances for weakness. If Sara should ever crack up herself she would get no sympathy from him. She had married an unforgiving man and she would have to stay strong to survive.

She showered and changed then lay down on the bed. She was much too worked up to sleep but she tried to relax, and, when she heard the door open and knew that Max was in the room, she lay still. She heard him moving around, although he always moved quietly and dark red Persian rugs covered most of the floor. But she went with him in her mind's eye as clearly as if her eyes were wide open and watching.

In the bathroom she saw him stripping, magnificently male, water cascading over his head, shoulders and back, down to the flat belly and the long, strong legs. Then he was towelling himself dry, and she knew his naked body almost as well as she knew her own. Skin-deep she knew him, but no deeper, although now, feigning sleep, she was sensually aware of his every move.

'Are you coming down or would you like something brought up here?' His voice was not raised, he was not trying to wake her; he knew she was not sleeping. She gave up pretending but she did not turn to look at him.

'What will your tame lawyer think if I don't go down?' she muttered. 'That I can't face him? That I'm sulking?'

'Sulking isn't your style.' It certainly was not his; he sounded amused. 'And don't worry about shocking Douglas. He's dealt with much bigger villains than young Jeremy.'

'But they weren't your brother-in-law.'

'Douglas's brother is doing five years for a multi-million-pound fraud on a leisure centre.'

She gasped. 'Was Douglas—?'

'Involved? No, and neither was I, if that was your next question, but it gives him a fellow feeling for those with a black sheep in the family. And Jeremy is less a black sheep than a slightly soiled lamb.'

That made the lawyer seem more human and spending a few hours with him less of an ordeal. She got off the bed as Max said, 'Choose one of these.' He took a flat black leather box from the top of the writing desk by the window and handed it to her. When she opened it she sagged back on the edge of the bed, swallowing a gasp.

'Wow! Are they real?' He didn't need to answer that; the stones blazed like white fire in their black velvet setting. Three rings. All diamonds. Three shapes, a central stone surrounded by smaller gems—marquise, square and round, known as brilliant. Sara stared at them speechless, although this was not a personal gift so much as fitting her out as Max Vella's wife.

Max said, 'If you don't like them you can see another selection tomorrow.'

'May I have this one?'

'Your choice,' he said. She put the ring on her finger herself. Until then her wedding band had been her only ring, and she remembered how strange she had felt when Max had put that on her finger. You have the option of walking away, he had told her, but with that ring he had left her with no escape.

It would take a while before she was used to the weight and the brilliance of the diamond on her finger. Later as she sat at the table with Max and Douglas Druitt the ring caught reflected light from wall brackets and side lamps, so that it seemed to be flashing every time she moved her hand.

It was quiet in this room, peaceful. Heavy brocade drapes were drawn across the windows. Outside the weather could be worsening, and the news of her marriage to Max Vella would be stirring a little storm of gossip. Several times she heard the faint ringing of phones, but in here they were not disturbed.

Half the time she was hardly listening, wondering what she was going to do about Beth and the children, as the men discussed horses at the stables of a local trainer they both knew. And then a climbing accident in the Himalayas that had happened to somebody else whose name meant nothing to Sara. But after that they began to talk about an archaeological dig from which the lawyer had just returned and Sara began to listen.

'My hobby,' said the lawyer, almost apologetically, and she would never have guessed that he had a hobby that could involve pick-and-shovel slog. She tried to imagine him looking scruffy, which made her smile.

'I'd love to do something like that.' She leaned towards him, and getting the full force of glowing amber green-flecked eyes in an enchantingly pretty face, the lawyer said, 'You'd be very welcome. In April—'

'I think not,' Max said curtly. 'Sara will be fully occupied here for the foreseeable future.'

And Douglas Druitt hurried to agree. 'Of course, I do realise that.'

So do I realise, thought Sara sourly, that Max intends getting value for money. For the rest of the meal she hid her resentment behind a bland, smiling mask of a face but when the lawyer had gone to one of the guest rooms and Sara and Max were alone in their bedroom she burst out, 'Why can't I go on a dig in April?'

'Because as my wife you'll be needed here.'

'Twenty-four hours a day, seven days a week?'

'Ours is an arranged marriage.'

'I'm not likely to forget the arrangement that you'd settle my family's debts—with conditions I didn't know about at the time—but I didn't realise I'd be under orders for the rest of my life.'

'Now you're being melodramatic.'

He sounded as if he was talking to a child, and she shrilled, 'It's been a melodramatic day. When you told Jeremy he'd get worse than broken legs if he welshed on you, that sounded pretty threatening to me. What did you have in mind? Breaking his neck? His back? Putting him in a wooden box rather than a wheelchair?'

'Murder, you mean?'

Now he was laughing at her, but the words jerked out. 'Could you commit murder?'

'Most people could.'

'I couldn't.'

'Let's hope you're never put to the test.'

He was not taking this seriously, and she supposed it had been a stupid question. She said tartly, 'Any other rules of conduct for me?'

'One other thing—don't amuse yourself with Douglas. Like most men he's flattered when a pretty woman flirts with him.'

It took a few seconds to get her breath back. 'I was not flirting.'

'Then what exactly were you doing?'

'I was—' Surely it was obvious? 'I was asking questions because I was interested. What do you think I was doing, propositioning the poor little man?'

'If you didn't realise the effect you were having you're an idiot,' Max drawled. 'But from now on any man who tries to take you up on that will be an even bigger fool.'

She gave a hoot of mocking laughter. 'Oh, I'm sure they'll be realising that. Nobody would dare make free with your property.'

'Never more than once,' he said, and he went into the dressing room, closing the door behind him.

He had not denied he considered her his property. The rules were all his rules, and if she had to fight every inch of the way what kind of a life would that be? Battling on when already she was beginning to feel bruised and battered.

The phone began to ring on the desk by the window. She picked it up slowly and said, 'Hello.'

'Mrs Vella? Mrs Max Vella?'

'Er—yes.' It was the first time she had answered a phone to that name. It would have seemed more natural to say 'Sara Solway'.

The voice was a woman's, throaty, husky. 'Make hay while the sun shines, sweetie; it's going to be a long, hard winter.'

The line went dead and Sara said into her silent receiver, 'Whoever you are, sweetie, you took the words right out of my head.' And on the dark glass of the window pane she saw the first white flakes of snow.

CHAPTER SIX

SARA was still staring at the phone when Max came back into the room. He asked 'Who was the caller?'

She said, 'They rang off.'

It could have been for him. It must have been put through to this room from somewhere else in the house, and she said, 'You can always find out, but it was not my family.'

'It hasn't been much of a homecoming for you, has it?' Just a few minutes ago he had walked out on her looking and sounding as if he could turn into her enemy. This seemed like a different man.

'Like you said,' she said. 'It's been instructive.'

'Sorry about that.'

Her mouth fell open. 'That's not something you say often.'

'I can't remember the last time.' But when she tried to speak he said, 'I'm not going back on the financial condition, I'm interested to see how they'll react on that one, but about Douglas. You made his evening, and I was wrong to accuse you of stringing him along.'

'Yes, you were.'

'Truce?'

She didn't want antagonism. She was tired of struggling. She gave a small shrug. 'Why not?' But when he smiled a smile tugged at her lips and wid-

ened to a grin. 'Yes, please,' she said. Heaven knew
she wanted him on her side. Even when she came
close to hating him she wanted him.

'Come to bed,' he said, and a frisson of desire
quickened her blood. 'I'll let you sleep; you've had
enough hassle for one day.'

'Hassle, you call it?' she teased, and they both
were laughing.

Max was in bed before her. He held out his arms
and she nestled against him and lay quietly. He held
her gently, giving her a feeling of safety and com-
fort, as he had when he'd wrapped her into the
cashmere coat, and as she fell asleep in the cool
dark she thought, This is like coming home.

Sara's first day as mistress of the Moated House
was non-stop action. She started off in a highly
nervous state. When she tried to eat a continental
breakfast the coffee scalded the roof of her mouth
and the croissant crumbs stuck in her throat.
Douglas Druitt had already left for London and
Max was leaving after breakfast to attend a board
meeting up north. Sara had extended her leave at
work and now had to face the flood of questions
from friends and press.

'What shall I say?' she asked him. 'If I tell them
how sudden it was it's going to sound unbelievable.
I know what a story reporters would make of it.
Shall I say we've known each other a while and
we've been meeting in secret for about—six
months?'

'Six months it is,' he said. 'Don't answer personal questions. Just put on a Mona Lisa smile as if you're keeping all the secrets to yourself.'

'How do I do a Mona Lisa smile?' She tilted her head, half smiling with closed lips and half-closed eyes. 'Like this?'

'Very enigmatic,' he said. 'Mona on the smug side.'

They would all be expecting her to look smug—the hard-up girl who had caught the catch of the county. But when she was presented to the staff she didn't feel smug so much as ridiculous. Some of them were lined up in the hall to meet their new mistress, like a scene from period television—Mrs Thomson, the cook, the butler, the head gardener, three other men, two other women. Sara moved along with Max beside her, smiling and getting twitchy smiles in return because every one of them was clearly in a state of shock.

Sara was shocked when Max introduced her to Alison Perry. Alison looked a very successful career woman from the top of her well-cut hairstyle to the tip of her Gucci-type shoes. Her fitted beige suit looked like an Armani and her make-up was flawless. Large tinted glasses hid her eyes, but Sara would bet that she didn't miss a thing.

Alison was here to act as secretary-cum-minder to Sara. And as a spy reporting back to Max? Sara wondered. Those big dark glasses made you wonder what was going on behind them. 'Take it easy today. Let Alison take the flak.' Max kissed Sara lightly on the cheek. 'I'll be back around six this evening.'

Alison smiled and her teeth were perfect. So was she. Super-efficient, vetting phone calls, explaining diary dates where Sara might want to accompany Max, organising the collection of Sara's things, including her car, from her old flat. Lunchtime she went down to the kitchens and brought back a tray of light and healthy foods: soup, fruit, salad, cold cuts and quiches, and Sara half expected Alison would try to spoonfeed her.

Alison left at four, promising, 'I'll see you tomorrow.'

'That would be nice,' said Sara. She hadn't exactly warmed to Alison, but she guessed she should reckon herself lucky to get a girl Friday who would have had Crusoe kitted up and off that island by Wednesday.

Last night's snow hadn't settled, and as soon as Alison's car was out of the gates Sara was in her own car driving towards Beth and the twins. It would be a fleeting visit—giving the twins the presents she had promised they would have today and seeing for herself how Beth was. Sara was more than ready to play her part in this arranged marriage, but banishing her family had been an afterthought and a whim on Max's part and it was not on.

She parked in the little drive and rang the front doorbell. If there was no answer she would put a note through the letter box and leave the hobby-horses in the garden shed, but the door opened almost at once. The twins squealed and so did Beth.

Then Beth dragged Sara into the house, hissing, 'Does he know you're here?'

'Don't *worry*,' said Sara. 'You're not making contact, I am. But I can only stay a few minutes.'

Beth had a hundred questions to ask and Sara dodged most of them. 'It was sudden, but it's going to be all right. How's Jeremy?'

'Starting work today in a club where Max Vella has an interest,' Beth stammered.

Sara said, 'Don't look so doleful. Be happy for me. Be happy for us because we really were in big trouble.'

'I know that.' Beth had nearly killed herself rather than face the trouble they had been in. She was trying to smile now and not making too good a job of that either. 'And I am happy for you. It's just that I still can't believe it. It was so unexpected, such a shock.'

'Like a bolt from the blue,' Sara said cheerfully.

And, driving back to the Moated House, she thought, I was right there—it was a bolt from the blue. She was feeling much less cheerful than the impression she had tried to give Beth. Defying Max, in theory when she was sure she had right on her side, was all very well—getting away with it could be no laughing matter.

Max arrived home not long after Sara had left her car in the garage. She had gone up to their bedroom to decide what to wear this evening, for her first public appearance as his wife, when he walked into the room. 'How did the meeting go?' she asked.

'According to plan.' His plan of course. He loosened his tie, a relaxing gesture, but the lines on his face were still as deep. 'And your day? Did Alison cope?'

'Need you ask? How long can you spare her? She must have been running at least a couple of departments somewhere. Well a lot of people phoned and faxed. Alison took messages and gave out statements. I answered some calls. Friends thought it was some kind of joke, and when I said we'd been meeting for some time they decided I'd been holding out on them and some of them turned huffy. My mother...'

She could hardly have found her a more eligible son-in-law, but Francesca Solway's first reaction had been gibbering indignation. 'How could you, Sara? Run off and marry a man you'd never even mentioned before and not a word to your mother or your sister? It was very hurtful, very selfish. Beth is very upset...'

'My mother was surprised,' Sara said carefully.

Max had gone into the dressing room, listening to her garrulous account of her day through the open door. Then he said, 'How's your sister? I hope you didn't give her back the pills.'

Somehow he knew she had seen Beth, and this could mean he was withdrawing his support. 'You can't do that,' she whispered.

He knew what she meant. 'Don't underestimate what I can do,' he said.

She reached the doorway, feeling physically sick because she had only herself to blame. She said, 'If you put the screws on Jeremy because I went to see Beth that would be so unfair. This was my fault. They did nothing. I don't know what they would have decided, but Jeremy started work today, didn't he? So he's trying to pay what he owes you.'

Max had taken off his jacket and was pulling off his shirt as Sara asked, 'What are you going to do about them?'

'Nothing; you've blown that little test. Were you too much of a coward to wait and see?' he asked ironically.

She kept her chin up. 'I'm not a coward. I've never been a coward.' She would have been heart-broken if Max's bullying had kept her family from her but he hadn't been giving them much choice, and she blurted, 'Why were you so certain I'd be seeing Beth today?'

She was sure she had not been followed. She could think of no way he could have been told. His customary drawl was in his voice. 'Your life will be less complicated and much easier if you simply accept that I always know.'

There was something in his eyes, as if another man looked out, and something told her that, if she valued her health and happiness, she should avoid that man like the plague.

That evening they drove through a countryside glittering with frost to a gallery in a neighbouring town and a preview of an art exhibition. Sara knew the gallery and the fine arts shop. Their regular line was handling the work of established artists, but now and again they provided a showcase for prom-

ising newcomers and tonight was the start of a
month's showing of three young artists.

There was a fair-sized crowd there already, and
as soon as Max and Sara walked in Sara could spot
those who knew Max or herself. They were the
ones who stopped talking and turned to stare. The
rest chattered on but the noise level dropped as if
a volume control had been turned right down.

A plump, bearded man in a tuxedo came hurrying
towards them. The director of the gallery had met
Sara before and been amiable but nowhere as eager
as this time. Obviously Max was a valued customer,
and as Mrs Max Vella Sara would be getting the
same red-carpet treatment.

It started as soon as Max introduced her as his
wife, and the director bowed over her hand as
though she had turned into minor royalty. If she had
been her old self she would have enjoyed the exhibition, but tonight was different because tonight
she was on show herself.

She felt as if at least half of the guests were talking about her, and everywhere she looked she met
sharp eyes and got smiles ranging from a tic to a
grin. Some eyed from head to foot, and more than
once she heard them asking each other, 'Who *is*
she?'

Max bought a small sculpture in steel and a couple of impressionist paintings. Nothing that would
fit into the decor of the Moated House, but he had
other houses where Sara supposed they might be at
home. There was nothing patronising about him—

he was an appreciative buyer, leaving the artists looking pleased and proud.

The press was here too, not from the *Chronicle* but Tony Simpson from the staff of a news agency cornered Sara while Max was talking to someone else. 'You're a dark horse, aren't you? How long has this been going on?' Tony, short and stocky and a fussy dresser, leered at her.

'A few months,' she said demurely. His eyebrows went up and the corners of his mouth went down.

'Not long, then.' Tony sounded grudging. 'Married life seems to be suiting you.' She could see Max at the centre of a group, broad shoulders and boxer's biceps beneath the sharp well-cut jacket, and felt her body melting like a young girl lusting from afar for a man she hardly knew. 'He's had some gorgeous women in his time,' said Tony.

'But I am the one he married.'

'Last time I saw him,' said Tony. 'Only about a couple of months ago, that was, he was with one of the most beautiful women I've ever seen. Sexy as hell with huge violet eyes. And they never took their eyes off each other. Still, like you say, you are the one he married.' She did her Mona Lisa smile and felt a sharp little stab that had to be jealousy. My stars, she thought, I must watch that never gets worse.

That week the Vella marriage was hot news. On Wednesday there was a paragraph on the gossip page of a national tabloid.

Spotted on Monday at an art exhibition—tycoon Max Vella and his very new bride, flame-haired twenty-three-year-old journalist Sara Solway. Sara is a surprise winner in the Vella matrimonial stakes, pipping several likely runners at the post. The only previous sighting of Vella and Sara together was at a fifth of November ball held at his manor house in the Midlands, where they were, according to one reveller, very much an item. But the bride's mother and Max Vella's wide circle of friends had no idea marriage was mooted until the happy pair returned from holiday last weekend, declaring themselves man and wife.

Sara read that over the breakfast table and pushed it across to Max. 'This will save us having to make an announcement,' he said. There was no need for announcements. Word of mouth was enough, reaching far and wide. The elopement was going to be hot local gossip until another scandal or rumour took the limelight.

Meanwhile Sara's mother was adapting to having Max as a son-in-law and her debts settled. Beth went shopping with Sara, to the theatre, to parties. She brought the children to the Moated House, usually to play in the grounds and gardens because when they were careering around in the house Beth was always waiting for them to knock over a Ming vase. 'I know they're going to smash something priceless,' she told Sara. 'And I'd never dare face Mrs Thompson let alone your husband.'

Beth was still in awe of Max. She kept out of

his way, but he had raised no further objections to
Sara seeing her family and her old friends. The arranged marriage was off to a good start. Groomed
and gowned by the best, Sara looked luminously
lovely, basking in Max's approval and support
everywhere they went.

He spoiled her with the skill of his lovemaking
so that she could never want any other man. Sometimes she tried to stay conscious of where the trail
of kisses and caresses brought the fiercest pleasure
until she reached her shattering climax—which she
always did. He was her husband, but that contract
had little to do with this. This was pure chemistry
and it was sensational.

He spoiled her with gifts too. Mostly jewellery,
but at Christmas there was a lovely unexpected
thing. A dolls' house they had seen where they had
bought the hobbyhorses was waiting in her bedroom on Christmas morning. Her family and some
of Max's friends were staying at the Moated House
for Christmas, with gifts for everyone piled beneath
a giant tree that reached as high as the gallery in
the main hall, but Sara's lit-up dolls' house was her
treasure.

The twins were allowed to view it as a peepshow
through the windows, because everything in there
was fragile and anything that got into the twins'
hands would probably disintegrate. So they looked
and marvelled, and Sara promised when they were
older—in about ten years' time, she thought—they
could play with it. She would be playing with it
herself, rearranging the rooms, marvelling at the

craftsmanship. She was thrilled with it and touched that Max should remember.

She was the hostess this Christmas for the small party gathered here, and the day after Boxing Day she sat at dinner with Max and three of his business colleagues. Afterwards she left them talking business. They would be leaving later when Max might, as he usually did, work later still in his study.

Sara had the next big event for the Moated House—next week's New Year's Eve Ball—on her mind. She decided to have an early night, and sat up in bed studying the guest list. Some names she knew, most she did not, and any of the unknowns could be the most beautiful woman Tony had mentioned.

She had met many attractive women in the weeks since she'd become his wife, some of whom tried to flirt blatantly with him. She always looked them in the face but none of them had the violet eyes Tony had mentioned, so she smiled when they hinted, and went deaf if they got out-and-out bitchy. Then she would overhear them telling each other, 'That girl is so *thick*.'

Some time Sara was bound to meet the sexy one with the violet eyes. She kept telling herself that Max had said he was tired of playing the field, he wanted a wife, he had chosen Sara, and his past was none of her concern. She remembered that first little stab of jealousy. That had been a warning.

She fell asleep thinking of the ball, the dresses she and Beth had chosen on one of Sara's accounts. The silk underwear. Since Max had awoken Sara's sensuality she was easier in her skin. She enjoyed the feel of nakedness between the sheets and no longer wore nightwear. The room was warm, the bed pleasantly cool, and she slept peacefully until she jerked from deep slumber to stark wakefulness.

At no time did she think this was her own heart beating or a clock ticking. The sound was unmistakable—it was a galloping horse and she reached blindly for Max. He was not in the bed. She was alone and the pounding hoofbeats were coming closer...

She woke with a start and told Max about her dream.

He said, 'We're going outside.'

'Where?' She was clammy all over.

'To the stables; where else would you expect to find a horse?'

But that had been a dream. She dressed clumsily, her chilled fingers fumbling with zips and buttons, while Max waited impatiently, and as soon as she got a coat on he took her arm and hurried her down the stairs that led to the back of the house, the courtyard and the outhouses.

Out here lights were on and there was a little flurry of activity. A door in the old stable block was open and there was a black horse in one of the stalls. A horse, and a man, small and wiry enough to be a jockey, who was grinning from ear to ear.

'Isn't she a beauty?' said the little man, stroking the gleaming neck.

'She's real, she's not a dream,' Sara whispered.

'That was the idea,' said Max.

He had ordered a black horse, replacing the horse Sara had had as a teenager, from the local stables. A groom was delivering it, latish, but he would be living here from now on and several of the staff were acting as a welcoming committee.

Sara adored her horse on sight. It could have been Black Bess, and it would be wonderful to ride over the hills again. Max could not have given her anything that would have pleased her more. 'Thank you,' she said. 'Oh, thank you. I'm only sorry I panicked like that. I only wish you'd warned me.'

'It was meant to be a surprise,' Max said drily, as they turned back to the house.

New Year's Eve at the Moated House was always a private party, by invitation only. More select than the Bonfire night Ball, but the guest list was well over a hundred. All Sara had to do this time was leave the preparations to professional firms that had been here before, and to Mrs Thomson who had overseen galas galore. She would be personally involved planning future events but at this party Sara's role was to show them all that, after less than two months, Max Vella's wife could put on a class act as lady of the manor.

The mid-November snow flurries had petered out in days. There had been no white Christmas, just a cold wind blowing under overcast skies, but on the morning of New Year's Eve snow began falling again and by evening the Moated House and the world around were shimmering like a winter palace in a fairytale.

Beth and Jeremy arrived among the earlier
guests, as beautiful a pair as any of the beautiful
people. Jeremy in a midnight-blue velvet suit, and
Beth in an empire-style dress and a triple pearl
choker. The pearls were real, one of Max's gifts to
Sara, and Beth had insisted Sara got Max's permis-
sion before she would borrow them. 'Why should
I mind?' he'd said. 'You can do what you like with
them.'

Jeremy was doing well at the club, and Sara
kissed him as well as Beth, in a sisterly fashion.
'My, you're looking handsome,' she said, and to
Beth, 'And you are so pretty.'

Inside the great house had been transformed into
vistas of glittering grottoes. 'It's like a fairytale isn't
it?' said Beth.

'Tonight it surely is,' said Sara.

Whatever Max's friends thought about the secret
wedding, Sara was not letting him down. Her dress
was off the shoulders and full-skirted in oyster
satin. She was wearing exquisite antique earrings
and a matching collar that showed off her smooth
white throat and the rise and fall of firm young
breasts. She looked like a princess, and felt like one.

The party was in full swing when half a dozen
latecomers came, waving and weaving their way
through the throng, to be greeted by Max and introduced to Sara. Four prosperous-looking men and
two expensive-looking women. Sara murmured
something suitable, and when other guests they
knew drew them away one woman stayed. She was
smiling into Max's eyes, and Sara blinked, seeing

this face in a sea of faces as if it had suddenly come into focus. The rooms were full of glamorous guests, but this girl would be a star anywhere.

She was ravishing. About Sara's age, with a perfect heart-shaped face, smooth, shining black hair reaching halfway down her back and incredible violet eyes. Her short, skimpy silver dress clung like a second skin, and she had the height and figure of a top model. It seemed to Sara as if a glass wall came down, shutting off Max and this girl from the rest of the company, and that if she herself tried to touch him she would encounter a cold, hard barrier. Only the girl could reach him now, her long silver-tipped fingers gripping so hard that he must feel their pressure as if his arm was bare.

'You should have waited for me, Max,' she said, and her voice was husky, throaty. 'You should have remembered I always come back.'

Sara had heard much this sort of thing said before, from women who resented Max having married Sara, but this time it was different. This, she knew—and would have known even if the girl had been wearing contact lenses that turned her eyes blue—was the one.

'How are you, Imogen?' Max asked.

'As always,' she said, and he took her hand from his arm, holding it as Sara turned away and met Douglas Druitt's eyes. There was no mistaking the look of pity on the lawyer's face, and she had to talk to him. She moved towards him and asked, 'Can I speak to you in private?'

'Of course.' He could hardly say no, although he

might wish he could, and they walked out of the
main hall into one of the corridors. Sara opened a
door to a room that had not been included in the
party planning. She saw there was no one in there
and she closed the door behind them.

'It was Imogen you were expecting Max to marry
wasn't it?'

She didn't need it confirmed. Every instinct told
her that Max and this girl had been passionate lovers whether Douglas lied or not. 'Well…' he began,
and after a few seconds hesitation, 'Well—yes.'

'Do they all know about her?'

The person who had taken that call on Sara's first
night, had told Imogen about the shock marriage
and had put her through to their bedroom. Most of
the guests here tonight would probably find the
meeting of Max's ex and his surprise bride more
fun than the cabaret. But Douglas said, 'Very few.
Max is a complex and private man.'

Sara had always accepted that. It seemed that nobody knew Max well, including Druitt, but she
asked him the question that was never far out of
her mind. 'Why did he marry me?'

Douglas pursed his lips, a lawyer giving a considered opinion. 'Well, now, my belief is that
Imogen gave Max an ultimatum about marrying
her, but when he began thinking about marriage he
decided she was not the kind of wife he wanted.
Max, you see, is a natural leader who must always
be in control. Now Imogen is a wealthy woman and
she likes her own way. A woman who was dependent on him would suit Max better.'

Sara was certainly dependent, and she said wryly, 'That makes me sound a very boring second-best.'

'Certainly not.' Douglas rushed to reassure her. 'You are a charming, delightful young lady. And I may be a touch old-fashioned, but I find it a refreshing change to meet a biddable wife.'

'Biddable!' Sara echoed. She would not have called that a compliment, but it was how this middle-aged lawyer saw it.

He was smiling now, telling her, 'Max does not make mistakes; he has the right wife.'

'Kind of you to say so,' said Sara, and it was kind. He was a kind man who was talking rubbish—everyone made mistakes, even the high and mighty Max Vella and the flat-broke and biddable Sara Solway.

'Shall we join the others?' said Douglas, and escorted Sara back to the party, happily believing he had reassured her and that she was feeling better for their little chat.

It was a brilliant party. All Sara's friends thought it was a triumph for her, and some of the others were admitting she was a looker and she had a way with her and Max Vella was well-known for knowing what he was doing. But the girl in the silver dress, who was never far away from Max, was spoiling it all for Sara.

Sara and Max sat together for the cabaret, but Imogen sat next to Max on the other side and whispered in his ear while the international star was singing for his supper and a fat fee.

As the applause for the singer died down, a few

minutes before midnight, the first wail of the bag-pipes could be heard. A piper was patrolling the battlements and the haunting, unearthly music grew louder until he reached the Long Gallery that had been turned into a ballroom, a splendid red-bearded figure in full Highland regalia, striding out, kilt swishing, scarlet cheeks puffing ferociously.

Jeremy and Beth were sitting by Sara. It was be-cause they had Max on their side they were here, their problems solved, having the time of their lives. They owed everything to him. So did Sara. This marriage had bought her the clothes, the jewels, the lifestyle. But not Max. In no way did Max belong to her, and from now on, if she ever forgot that, Imogen would be around to remind her.

The chimes of midnight had everyone on their feet, hands clasped for the dance of Auld Lang Syne. 'Should auld acquaintance be forgot…' they sang, and in the mêlée of hugs and kisses, with everyone squealing happy New Year, Sara saw Imogen fling her arms around Max, hanging onto him, so that Sara seemed the outsider as Imogen greeted everyone with, 'Happy New Year, sweetie, a very happy New Year.'

Anyone walking in, knowing nobody, would have thought that Imogen was mistress here. She had been Max's mistress and she fully intended to be again. Sara did her share of kissing and never stopped smiling, because she had to get through the hours of drinking, dancing and merrymaking that still stretched ahead.

Beth was a belle of the ball and Jeremy was in

his element. Sara danced with him, and Jeremy was always like her father, a born charmer. His high spirits made Sara smile, and she was happy to see them so happy, while her mother seemed to have spent the whole evening in the company of a grey-haired, distinguished-looking man whose name Sara couldn't remember. She had met so many distinguished-looking men tonight.

Breakfast would be served at three o'clock, but just after two Francesca told Sara, 'Oh, I have enjoyed myself so much but I think I should go home now.' She yawned prettily. 'I'm not as young as I was.'

She waited for the grey-haired man to speak and he obliged, saying, 'Our hostess has to be your sister, you can't be her mother.'

'She was a child bride,' said Sara dryly, sure that her mother had told him that although Francesca had been twenty-four when she'd married.

'Thank Max for me,' Francesca gushed. 'I can't see him around. Will you tell him he's my very favourite son-in-law?'

'I'll tell him,' Sara promised. It would amuse him to hear her mother had decided he had the edge on Jeremy. The company had thinned out slightly and she should have spotted Max; he was the tallest man here. He was in none of the obvious places, but he could be going into rooms as she left them; the house was a maze of corridors and chambers.

She couldn't see Imogen either. There were other flashing silver dresses but none of them was Imogen's, and Sara found herself climbing a staircase that led to the top storey. Passages were lit up here; some of the rooms had been prepared for guests who were staying overnight.

When she opened one door the room was empty with a neatly turned-down bed. In the next room it was the same. Then she came to an archway with a narrow flight of stone steps leading up one of the towers. It was colder going up here; the stairway ended on the battlements. Near the top there was a room behind a heavy studded door which creaked as she opened it.

A little light came through a slit window; the room was in deep shadow, and for a moment she thought she saw shapes moving and that she had found Max and Imogen. She tore into the room like an avenging fury and within seconds she would have screamed, but the room was empty. The shapes were a chair, a table, a roll of carpet, and Sara stumbled out again, her outstretched hands feeling the rough walls to steady herself as she climbed the last few steps and came out onto the battlements.

She couldn't go back to the rooms below and the partygoers until she was calmer. It was too cold for there to be anyone else up here. She needed to be alone and she needed the bitter wind to cool the fever in her brain. She must have been out of her mind, because if she had found Max and Imogen in the darkness in that room she would have thrown herself between them, she would have carried on like a wild woman, so that she had no shred of dignity or reason left.

And what would have happened next was too awful to contemplate. Max would have held her off. There would have been no rage in him. Anger, yes, but it would have been controlled and contemptuous because she was no cheated wife. All her rights were in material things. Imogen would have laughed. Sara was sure that Imogen would have tossed back her long hair and laughed her husky laugh.

If, in one of these rooms behind a closed door, Max and Imogen were having an erotic reunion, Sara should be so thankful that she had not stumbled across them. There *were* things it was better not to know, and she must never lose control again as she so nearly had tonight.

She breathed in the icy air and then someone touched her, which made her spin round. It was Max. She was so startled she was incoherent, then she stammered, 'It's you.'

'Who were you expecting?' he drawled.

'Nobody—I—how did you know I was here?'

'I was told you'd been seen going into the tower. What do you think you're doing?'

She couldn't tell him what she'd thought she was doing. She said, 'I needed a few minutes alone.'

'Alone?' He seemed to be questioning that, although he could see she was alone. 'What's your problem? What's on your mind?'

The cold was inside her now, and when he asked, 'Are you regretting our bargain?' she might have asked, Are you? But he might have said yes, and she would need to be stronger before she could take that chance. She shook her head.

'Then get back to our guests,' he said curtly. He went ahead of her, down the narrow stone steps, and stood watching her until she reached another flight of stairs. Imogen had to have been waiting for him because five minutes later Sara saw her and Max together again across a crowded room.

He didn't need Sara to play hostess. Imogen was fitting the bill nicely but he was paying Sara to do the job, and Max Vella got what he paid for, so Sara circulated and smiled. Even when the full breakfast was served. Although how they could face eggs and bacon, kidneys and kippers and kedgeree, after the buffet they had been scoffing all night, was beyond her. The sight and the smell of it all made her stomach heave.

She went up to their bedroom when Beth and Jeremy went to theirs. 'It's been the loveliest night,' Beth said while Jeremy, more than slightly high on champagne, kissed Sara's hand. Max was still talking with other guests, and Sara thought, I won't be seeing you again till morning.

She had to accept that. She must not think about it. But when she was alone she found herself heaving her heart out, sick to her stomach. Rich food and excitement and everything else. Most of all knowing that Max would be in Imogen's bed somewhere in this house.

She got out of her finery—the satin dress and the jewellery. It was very late; she should be very tired. She must try to sleep, because tomorrow she would be on duty again, but she hadn't a hope of sleeping. Nor of stopping the pictures that were running through her brain like an erotic movie. This was a big room, but the walls seemed to be closing in on her as she paced up and down.

As dawn was beginning to break she gave up on sleep, dressed warmly and came downstairs. There were sounds that meant some of the clearing-up operations were under way, but most doors were closed. Guests still slept. Only a skeleton staff was around.

Sara met no one, and when she let herself out of the house the courtyard was deserted. In her stall Black Bess got to her feet and whinnied a welcome as Sara called her name. She had ridden the horse several times in the past week, and already there was an understanding between them. Sara had come out here to pet her and talk to her and give her an apple, but she had time to spare before the hungover guests would be surfacing and Max and Imogen would be putting in an appearance.

She would be expected to accept that placidly as a biddable wife when it would have taken very little to have had her shrieking, I hope your breakfast chokes you.

She must steady down; she reached for Bess's harness and saddle. There was snow on the ground but it was not deep and a gentle canter over the hills should be safe for the horse. If the going got rough, she would turn back.

It was a grey dawn but a white world so that an eerie light fell on them. Earlier snow had drifted into the valleys, making the terrain unfamiliar. She didn't climb into the saddle until they were through a gate leading onto the hills, and then she let Bess have her head, trotting along a pathway they had taken before. It could be another planet, Sara thought, and she wouldn't have minded if it had been. This world was becoming hellish. Going back to the Moated House would be grim. She wished she could gallop away, and she closed her eyes and laid her cheek against the horse's neck and imagined she was racing in a rush of speed, leaving it all behind her.

But they had to go back, and eventually and reluctantly she reined Bess in. Snowflakes were fluttering around like moths and Sara snapped out of her dark mood to take in the weather situation. It was snowing again, thickening as she stared, and in the few seconds it took her to turn the horse it was almost blowing a blizzard.

Bess could easily stumble in this and break a leg, and Sara dismounted, holding the reins. 'Home, Bess, we've gone too far.' The horse went with her, and they *had* gone too far because soon there was snow underfoot and blinding flakes whirling around them.

But it was not the horse that fell. It was Sara who put her foot in a rabbit hole and pitched forward, hitting her head on a boulder the snow had not sufficiently cushioned, and lay face down and unconscious.

CHAPTER SEVEN

SARA never knew how long she lay there before she was choking, snow filling her mouth and her eyes. When she lifted her head a white wave seemed to flow over her, and she fought for breath and tasted snow. Then she remembered where she was and what had happened—although the whirling whiteness was due as much to dizziness as the snowflakes falling around her. She sat up slowly, holding her head in both hands as if that might steady it, and called, 'Bess.' She must have let go of the reins when she'd fallen but the horse had to be near.

Her ankle hurt even through the numbing cold that was spreading through her whole body. She was wearing ankle boots, jeans, a thick sweater and a padded jacket, but she was not dressed warmly enough for this and she had to get moving. She banged her gloved hands together, feeling nothing except that her head was throbbing. She had no idea in which direction the house lay, nor where the roads were—there were miles of moorland out here.

She was so cold, and it *was* like another planet, without one familiar landmark. She was staggering around blindly but she had to keep moving, and pray that the snow would stop as suddenly as it had started. She called Bess again when she paused to take the weight off her foot, but there was no sign of the horse. She couldn't have broken her ankle or she couldn't be moving on it, but she had to have wrenched it pretty badly, and when she touched her forehead there was a hot and hurting spot on her frozen face.

She kept doggedly moving on, although she could be going round in circles. She knew the hills well but this was like trying to find your way through dense fog. It was worse than fog, obscuring the ground as well as the way ahead.

She was light-headed and, now, she was scared. When exhaustion and dizziness hit her together, and her ankle gave way, she stayed down, just for a few minutes, hunching herself into a tight ball, her hair spilling over her folded arms. 'Help me, Max,' she whimpered, and then she heard the helicopter and jerked her head back to stare up at the sky. The pain behind her eyes was fierce, but somehow she was on her feet, running around, waving her arms, screaming, 'I'm here, I'm here.'

Could a helicopter land on snow? How deep was it here? Her head was throbbing even when she closed her eyes and stopped waving and sank down again. Still calling, 'I'm here,' but no longer with the strength to scream.

Max reached her and the pain dulled when his arms were around her. She was going to faint but she managed to croak, 'Thank you very much.'

And she heard him say, 'You bloody fool,' as she passed out.

She came round again within minutes, still in

Max's arms, but now he was carrying her where there were a lot of people and a lot of noise. They were going upstairs, and her senses were coming back as far as seeing and hearing went. She knew she was in their bedroom, lying on the bed, while Mrs Thomson and another woman took off her boots and peeled off her clothes. She heard Mrs Thomson say, 'Soaked to the skin,' and heard Beth screaming, 'Sar, are you all right?' from what seemed a distance but had to be in the room.

I am paralysed, she thought, I can't move. But she was chilled to the bone, and sensation was coming back in agonising pins and needles. The other woman, a doctor still in the house among the overnight guests, was asking her, 'How are you feeling?'

'Fine,' Sara wheezed.

'Of course you're not fine,' Max snapped.

The doctor agreed with him. The ankle was puffing up and the lump on Sara's forehead seemed to concern the doctor. She shone pinpoints of light into Sara's pupils and asked her to follow the sidewards movements of a finger with her eyes, and put a thermometer under her tongue. Then she said, 'It's bed for you for a while. You get some rest; I'll get you something that will help.'

When Max left with the doctor there was no one left in the room but Beth and Mrs Thomson, who was going through a chest of drawers to find a nightgown for Sara. As an invalid she would be expected to be decently covered, although as she warmed up she was getting hotter. Beth helped her

into the nightdress. 'You're looking better,' Beth
declared. 'Isn't she looking better?' she asked Mrs
Thomson who looked at Sara's feverish face and
recognised a rising temperature when she saw one.

'I'll get her a hot drink.' She looked doubtfully
at Beth. 'Are you staying?'

'For now,' said Beth.

'Well keep it down,' said Mrs Thomson.

As soon as the door closed after her Sara asked,
'Keep what down? What's she talking about?'

Beth looked shamefaced. 'I made a bit of a fuss,
I suppose. When we couldn't find you, Jeremy went
to ask Max where you were and he said you were
around in the house somewhere, but he started looking then, and then the horse came back. It had been
snowing and Max went dashing off and the helicopter went up and you were out there.'

'I should have stayed with Bess if she found her
way home.'

'I was so scared,' said Beth.

'You and me both,' said Sara.

'But I went a bit hysterical, and when he came
back and he was carrying you you were so white,
you looked so awful I started screaming.' Beth's
eyelids were puffy, although she was smiling now
as she tried to brighten up. 'Anyhow it was a lovely
party. Those who hadn't gone home stayed on to
see if Max was going to find you. I suppose they'll
all be leaving now.'

And Imogen? Sara wondered. Was she with Max
this morning before they realised I was missing? Is
she still here? While I am lying helplessly in bed

will Imogen be helping Max in all sorts of ways? She said, 'I'm not feeling too bad; I'm going to get up.'

'He wouldn't like that.' Beth shuddered at the very idea of defying Max.

'I shall put on a housecoat and go downstairs where there are dozens of settees to lie on,' Sara said stubbornly, and she got off the bed, walking slowly, going easy on the ankle, reaching the clothes closet in the dressing room before the black waves began rolling over her.

Beth, who had hovered around protesting, screeched, 'Sar!' as Max came into the main room.

He roared, 'What the *hell*—?'

'I'm getting up,' Sara gasped as she fell. He picked her up without saying a word but he looked angry enough to be shaking her.

When Mrs Thomson appeared he snarled, 'Where have you been?' with such tight-lipped fury that she was speechless. 'She has concussion,' Max thundered. He put Sara back into the bed gently, and covered her with the bedclothes. 'For God's sake, woman, you must have realised it's essential she has no exertion at all? Why the blazes didn't you stay with her?'

The housekeeper held out the beaker and the small glass she was carrying and said, so meekly that Sara would not have recognised her voice, 'I was fetching these; her sister was here.' She frowned at Beth, but then sighed as if she should have known that Beth would be no use in an emergency.

Now Sara was lying down the walls had stopped going round. 'I insisted on getting up,' she croaked. 'Beth couldn't stop me. Mrs Thomson couldn't have.'

'Oh, yes, she could,' said Max, and he was right. In Sara's weakened state Mrs Thomson could have stopped her with one hand. Max could have done it with a word.

'Are you all right?' Mrs Thomson was asking her.

'Yes. I'm sorry.'

'And we'll have no more nonsense about getting up until the doctor says so?'

'No,' said Sara, and got a smile from the house-keeper for that.

'Go home, Beth,' Max said wearily, and Beth kissed Sara's cheek and crept out of the room with Mrs Thomson right behind her.

'Do I have bad concussion?' Sara asked Max fearfully. Her head still ached.

'Jenny doesn't think so but she isn't too happy about you.' He didn't look happy either. His scowl turned his dark brows into a straight, stern line. 'Trying to get up was lunatic. So was riding this morning; did the horse throw you?'

'No.' Beth had just been blamed for Sara's reck-lessness; she didn't want Bess tagged as the cause of her wandering all by herself in the snow. 'I got off and tried to walk. When I slipped and screamed it must have spooked her. She came home?' He nodded. 'I'm so glad; is she all right?'

'Better than you,' he said grimly. 'What got into you? What did you think you were doing?'

Putting off seeing you and Imogen together again, she thought. She said meekly, 'It wasn't snowing then; it came on so suddenly.'

'You weren't even wearing a riding hat.' That had been another incredibly stupid thing. She didn't need to be told. 'If you had been you might not have hit your head. Although,' he said, 'if it hadn't been for your hair you'd have been harder to spot. The snow was easing off but you were in a white jacket, and it was this—' he touched a damp tendril of her hair '—that I saw.'

As always she got a little charge of energy from his touch so that she looked up wide-eyed as he glared down. 'You do realise you came damn close to the edge?' His smile was softening his hard face, and suddenly her eyes were filling with tears and she had to sniff before she could speak.

'I thought I might be out there for hours, that nobody would miss me.'

'Small chance of that,' he said. 'You were missed.'

She liked hearing him say that.

'Here, drink this.' He was holding the beaker to her lips, and she gulped the warm, sweet drink. 'Now this.' The small glass. She swallowed obediently, then started coughing.

'What's this going to do?'

'Keep you where you should be.'

Like coming home, she thought drowsily. She was dead tired and the drug must have been strong;

as she was falling asleep she thought that he kissed her. Unless it was her hair falling across her cheek.

She woke, sneezing and burning hot. Curtains were drawn and a side lamp threw a mellow light. A fire burned in the white marble fireplace and Max sat by the lamp. He had been reading a book but now he was getting up out of the chair, and she croaked, 'Just what have I done to myself?'

'Nothing that a few days' doing as you're told won't put right,' he said.

'I feel horrible.'

'Serves you right.' He was smiling at her. She asked, 'What are you doing here?'

'Waiting for you to wake up. I don't want you staggering downstairs. It might be slight concussion but it's bed rest for the first twenty-four hours at least. That will keep your ankle out of trouble and get your temperature down.'

Even if Imogen was still in the house, he must have stayed near to Sara all day and all night. When her dreams had been delirious, she'd woken sobbing, shaking in every limb, and Max had been there to bring her out of her nightmares, cooling her temples with Mrs Thomson's lavender water, stroking her hair. He had been gentle and caring and she had felt safer with him than she had ever been.

Sara knew her temperature was high, but she wished that Max would stay on the bed beside her, and risk catching her feverish chill or whatever, rather than going back to his couch.

He was good to her while she was recovering.

The best. Nearly everybody was friendly and considerate. Flowers were being delivered from friends and guests from the party. Mrs Thomson turned out to be a first-rate nurse, and delicious dishes came up from the kitchens as Sara progressed from struggling to get down more than a mouthful to managing small portions.

Until all risk of concussion had gone she was allowed no visitors and no phone calls. She didn't mind much. She was not up to callers, nor trying to explain why she had gone riding into a snowstorm.

That was what everyone would be wondering. After the third day, when Sara was allowed visitors, Beth came, bringing Sara's pearls and their mother. Francesca brought the newspaper and there was a paragraph on the gossip page…

Tycoon Max Vella's recently wed wife was an enchanting hostess to more than a hundred guests at a convivial New Year's Eve party. But, come morning, Max's helicopter was searching for his bride over the moors surrounding the Moated House. Flame-haired Sara had gone horse riding alone into this winter's worst snowstorm so far—could that be a drastic cure for a hangover? Happily both horse and Sara were recovered. The horse none the worse, Sara with a heavy chill, and a sprained ankle.

Everybody would have seen this. Max laughed it off although Sara did not find it very funny. Each day she was feeling stronger. She still tired easily, but on the fifth day when Alison Perry turned up with her briefcase Sara managed to deal with some of the letters and papers she'd brought. As always Alison was wearing the big dark glasses, but Sara knew that behind them her eyes were cool. Her manner certainly was. She asked about Sara's health but she didn't bother to hide her opinion that Sara was a pain in the neck who didn't appreciate her own good fortune.

Sara hadn't had a headache in the last three days, but after an hour with Alison one was starting up again and she said, 'I'm sorry, but that's enough for now; do you mind?'

Alison put papers back in her briefcase. 'Not at all,' she said. 'You should know your limitations.' She slipped her arms into the scarlet topcoat she had thrown over a chair and left Sara with a chilly little nod.

Max was not here today and Sara was missing him. She always missed him now when he was away from her because she realised she was falling in love with him. When she was strong and healthy again she would remember how marvellous he had been when she'd needed tenderness, and she would go on falling in love. Her feelings for Max had changed dramatically. They were deeper, so much warmer. Nobody knew better than Sara how love could hurt, but these last days and nights had shown her that Max was a man worth loving. She wanted Max here so she could say, 'I love you.' If he ever said that to her, the man who never said the word love, she felt she would go crazy from happiness.

Imogen no longer worried her. She had pushed Imogen to the back of her mind like a bad dream. Her accident had been a blessing in disguise, and she couldn't wait for Max to come home. But the day that had started badly with Alison got worse in the afternoon with Beth and the twins. It was the twins' first visit since Sara's accident and they were brought up to her bedroom by Mrs Thomson.

Sara was still under doctor's orders to rest each afternoon, and she was lying on the Chesterfield in her bedroom. Beth was carrying one hobbyhorse, Mrs Thomson the other, and the twins trotted before them, looking angelic.

Beth said, 'They *would* bring them.'

'My Bess wants to say hello to Auntie Sar's Bess,' said Joanne. 'My Bess could find her way home if she got lost in a storm.' Joanne had the hobbyhorse with the silky black head.

'You be careful with those,' Mrs Thomson warned them.

Sara said, 'No riding in the house. We'll all go down to the stables after tea.'

They had tea in the little parlour—the cook did them proud as she always did—and then they went down to visit Black Bess in her stall and feed her with carrot sticks. All was well with Beth; Jeremy was working hard, she said, and he sent his love to Sara.

'You know I still can't believe that you're mistress of all this,' Beth said as they left the stables. 'Wasn't it a wonderful party?'

They reached the Long Gallery that had been the ballroom. On New Year's Eve it had been garlanded in ice-white and silver, and crowded with dancers. It was empty now, the gleaming floor stretching the width of the house, marble statues in niches, vases and porcelain pieces on pedestals.

At one of the long windows the sisters looked out over gardens where night was beginning to fall. Snow still lay out there, and Beth shivered. 'I still get the creeps when I think of you out on the hills and how you looked when he carried you back.'

'Don't think about it,' Sara advised. They stood a moment longer, looking out, then Beth turned her head and screamed, 'You stop that.'

The twins were racing the hobbyhorses down the gallery, their little legs working like pistons. 'Stop it,' Sara shrieked as they both reached the end of the gallery, and, unable to stop, crashed headlong into a Chippendale table and a pair of rare Worcester vases.

'Oh, no, oh, God, no,' Sara sobbed, running, and knowing she was too late to do anything. Of course, they were smashed. Pink and gold pieces lay by the upturned table, but she went down on her knees and went on praying, 'Oh, please *no*.'

The twins started keening together and Beth's breath was coming in panicky gasps. One vase seemed to have escaped. Sara hardly dared pick it up but when she turned it in her hands there seemed to be no chips, although there could be hairline cracks. The matching vase was in at least twenty pieces.

'Were they—very valuable?' Beth was whispering, and Sara knew she was nearly hysterical when she wanted to say, Fifty pence from a boot fair. She did say, 'They're two hundred years old, and there probably isn't another pair in the world like them.' Then wished she hadn't because Beth was making as much noise as the twins.

'I knew this would happen,' Beth howled. 'Didn't I say if they came in here they'd smash a Ming vase?'

After a few seconds Sara said, 'For pity's sake shut up. Look, you go home and I'll fix it.'

'You don't mean mend it?' Beth said incredulously, and Sara's patience was wearing thin.

She said, 'Yeah, with a tube of superglue. How do you think I could mend it?' She took Beth's arm and said in a lowered voice, 'I'll say I did it, that I felt dizzy again, and my ankle is still weak. Get them home now and don't let Max find out what happened for at least a month. Better still, never.'

'Are you sure?' But Beth would almost rather have faced a hungry tiger than an angry Max Vella. Sara picked up the hobbyhorses and then took Beth and the children out to their car. In the back seat Joanne cradled her horse's head, whispering to it, 'It wasn't your fault.'

'Are you safe to drive?' Sara asked Beth.

'Oh, *yes*!' Beth grabbed the wheel, switched on the ignition and took off down the long drive as if the hungry tiger were after her.

Sara dared not wait to see them go before hurrying herself, back to the Long Gallery. The broken vase could be found at any time and she would have to face the music, but she would delay the discovery if she could. Mrs Thomson had already cast a wary eye on the hobbyhorses. It would be better if she believed the accident had happened after the galloping twins had left.

There was still no one in the gallery, and Sara righted the table and began gathering up the pieces. A sharp sliver cut her as she grabbed it, and she watched a bead of blood welling on her fingertip. After that she tried to go less frantically but she was almost as shaken as Beth had been.

She didn't know how Max would react when he heard that an irreplaceable vase had been smashed. It could be mended, of course. Experts could put anything together. But it would never be the same, never be worth a fraction of its original value. She couldn't think how the second vase had escaped, although when she set that back on the table she would not have been surprised if it had fallen apart.

She put the pieces in the table drawer and stood, breathing fast, as if she had been running a race. Tonight she had meant to be downstairs when Max came home, but after this she felt no stronger than she had days ago, and she went back to her bedroom, back to the Chesterfield that Max had used as a bed after her accident. Last night he had slept in the little bedroom leading off the study, but tonight she thought he might be sharing her bed again.

Pillow talk was supposed to be a favourite ploy for wives who had a tricky subject to broach but Sara couldn't see herself, after making love, saying, By the way I've broken a vase. The other one's all right but they'll never be a matching pair again.

When there was a tap on the door she called 'Come in,' and sat up, waiting for Mrs Thomson to walk in and report a missing vase. But it was not Mrs Thomson, it was one of the maids, carrying a cellophane box.

'More flowers,' said Lucy.

This was an orchid, a wax-like flower with purple petals. There was no card in the box and Sara asked, 'Was there a message?'

'No, it's just been delivered.'

Max might have sent it, Sara thought, or someone would be phoning to ask if she had received it. She had been writing thank-you notes all week for flowers sent. It had been kind of friends who had remembered her like this, although there were flowers in the hothouses of the Moated House. 'I've never had an orchid,' Sara said. 'What do you do with them?'

'Some people wear them,' said Lucy. But Sara was not the type to have an orchid pinned on her. Lucy stood for a moment, then she said, 'Your sister's gone, then?'

'A while ago,' said Sara.

'Nice children,' said Lucy. 'Well behaved.'

'Yes,' said Sara, and thought, If only you knew...

She was getting more and more nervous, waiting

for Max. He had thought she was getting up and about too soon. When she told him she'd felt dizzy and had lurched against the table that would prove his point. If she tried walking round now she could fall all over the place because her head was whirling and her stomach was churning. Time was dragging, and when he did walk in she felt sick with apprehension.

'What's wrong?' he asked as soon as he saw her.

She had to get it over, and she plunged in. 'I've got a confession to make. I've broken one of the pink lustre vases in the Long Gallery. I knocked against the table.'

He had picked up the orchid, and she quavered, 'Did you send me that?'

'No, I did not. You knocked the table and a vase fell off; how badly is it broken?'

She swallowed the lump in her throat. 'It's smashed; it's in little pieces.'

'You crashed into the table?' A wheel of a hobbyhorse might have gone over the vase. It was a wonder the children weren't cut.

'Yes.' She didn't look at him, but she knew he had put the orchid in its box back on the table and that he had his back to her. He didn't turn when he spoke.

'Beth and the twins came this afternoon, I hear, and brought the hobbyhorses with them.'

'Yes.'

'Hobbyhorses in the Long Gallery?' Somebody had mentioned the visit, and Sara couldn't be sure nobody had seen them going into the gallery. 'A more likely scenario to me,' Max went on, 'is the twins crashing into the table.' Simply accept that I always know, he had told her.

Her, 'No,' came out as a squeak, but then he was looking at her, and of course he could find out. He'd only have to question Beth or the children.

'So why are you taking the blame?' he demanded.

Because her instincts always had been to protect them, and she said wretchedly, 'I thought it would sound better if it was my accident.'

'Your sister didn't need much persuading. She nearly ran into Higgins driving through the gates.' Higgins was one of the gardeners. 'Going like a bat out of hell, he said.' They had to have reached home safely; it had been hours ago. Sara would have heard by now if they hadn't. 'You constantly surprise and appall me, and that takes some doing. Don't lie to me again,' he said. His anger shrivelled her. 'Never lie to me again.' His voice was tight with suppressed violence, so close, so terribly close to explosion.

Then he turned abruptly and left the room, and she did not know whether it was the lie or the breakage or both that had enraged him, but she hoped he would not come back until the rage and the violence had burned themselves out. Because all of it seemed to be directed at her.

She did not see Max again that night. One of the maids brought up a tray of food, and Sara stayed in her room, drained in body and mind. But when she tried to sleep she couldn't shut out that threatening image, and she got out of bed to find Beth's sleeping pills at the back of a drawer in her dressing table. She swallowed a couple of them. The pills let her sleep until Lucy pulled the curtains. It was half past ten, and Sara raised heavy eyelids, still half asleep.

She reached for the cup of tea on her bedside table, mumbling thanks, and Lucy said, 'Mrs Thomson said we should be waking you, although before he left he said to let you rest. He left you a note.'

There was a note on the bedside table in Max's heavy black writing. 'If you feel up to it we might go out for a meal tonight,' Sara read. 'The two of us, somewhere quiet. A change of scene for you. Don't worry about the vase. Accidents happen.'

She read it again. And again. And each time it sounded better, so that at the last reading she was smiling. This was a peace offering, and she could understand why he had gone ballistic over the vase being broken and her silly excuse to keep the twins out of trouble. She badly wanted everything to be forgiven and forgotten. She desperately wanted a date tonight, just the two of them, when she would be sexy and beautiful and dressed to kill. And he would be sexy and handsome and a man to kill for.

She sang in the shower and danced around the room, dressed in designer trousers and a creamy silk shirt, wondering what she could wear tonight. She wished he had given her some idea where they were going. She could ask him of course when she saw him, and in the meantime she had fun considering smart little suits and elegant gowns. And jew-ellery. She took out rings, bracelets and necklets, then put most of them away again and spent another half-hour trying out new nail colours.

She made a few phone calls, getting no reply from Beth's number, and wrote two letters to old friends. But she was enjoying herself, up here alone, planning and waiting, excited as a girl on her first date. After the scene over the vase she had almost believed that their marriage was breaking up too. Now everything was wonderful again.

She might wear her hair up. She had a brilliant hairdresser but she was quite handy with hairstyles herself, and she was sitting in front of the mirror, pinning up a hank of hair, when the door opened and a fair head peered round. 'Gotcha,' said Jeremy.

Her brother-in-law was way down the list of Sara's favourite visitors, but she was quite fond of him now he was behaving himself. She put down the comb and said, 'Hello, what are you do-ing here?'

'Shh.' Jeremy did a pantomime silencing. 'I just walked in; there's not much security in this place.' Doors were left open during the day, but there was always staff around. If Jeremy had got up here with-out being spotted he had probably dodged a few of them. 'Beth said you were always in this room in the afternoons.'

'Usually,' said Sara. 'What do you want?'

'She's worried about the vase.' He rolled his eyes. 'How did it go?'

'It didn't go too badly,' Sara said.

'He is all right with you?' Jeremy didn't usually concern himself with other peoples' health.

'He's more than all right with me,' she said.

'I suppose he does see you right for cash?' Jeremy's boyish face was sly in spite of his winsome smile, and Sara glared at him.

'You can't be in debt again?'

'No way.' Jeremy was cut to the quick. But he didn't meet her eyes, and then he added, 'But I could use a loan; cash is tight.'

'No,' said Sara, and her no was louder than his. Jeremy liked the lavish lifestyle; cutting out luxuries would irk him.

'Fair enough,' he said, and Sara got up and walked away. She must not lose her temper. Another disturbing thought struck her. 'You are still at the club?'

'Of course I am; the club isn't bad. Plenty going on, plenty of talent.' She couldn't start lecturing him about keeping clear of the talent, and he began to tell her some quite funny stories, so that for a few minutes they were laughing together.

'Better get back,' he said, glancing at his watch. Sara was not keeping him, although as they went along the gallery towards the main staircase he held back and said, 'Can't we use another way? I should be at work; I cleared off for half an hour.'

'That's your problem,' she said, and then she saw Max and another man in the hall below. At the same time Max looked up and Jeremy groaned, and she got the impression Jeremy might be going to run as Max came up the stairs towards them.

Jeremy stayed but he was looking very uncomfortable, and Max said curtly, 'What can we do for you?'

'Just dropped in to see Sar,' said Jeremy.

'Well now you've seen her.'

'Yes,' said Jeremy. 'Yes.' He went down the stairs fast, past the man in the hall, out through the big door.

'What did he want?' Max asked Sara. She didn't want to set Max on him. Max disliked Jeremy as much as Jeremy feared Max.

'He just called in,' she said. That was no lie, although Jeremy had tried to get in and out of the house without being spotted and he had come to ask for money, even if he had given up easily when Sara had refused.

Max was looking suspiciously as if he might insist on her repeating every word of their conversation, but he said, 'Go and rest; you're still convalescing.' And she was glad to get away.

She lay down on the bed, feeling convalescent, although she had been fit enough until Jeremy had breezed in. She tried to relax, to think of Max and stop bothering about Jeremy. She dozed for a while and woke refreshed until she remembered Jeremy and the unholy mess he—like her father—had managed to make of life. Both of them cheated. Neither could be trusted. In his last job, before the club, Jeremy had had his fingers in the till. He'd always picked up bits and pieces as he had gone along.

Once it had been a friend's brooch that had vanished, a wallet at the cricket club. Nothing had been proved, but Sara knew that nobody could trust Jeremy with anything that wasn't nailed down.

'Oh!' She clapped her hand across her mouth and got off the bed, keeping her mouth gagged until she reached the dressing table. Then, looking down at the jewellery lying there, her fingers fell away and the words jerked out. 'You despicable little rat.' Jeremy had taken the brilliant.

The second her back had been turned he probably hadn't been able to help himself, it would have stuck to his fingers. No wonder he'd panicked when he'd seen Max. Once out of the house he stood a chance of getting away with it, knowing Sara would miss the ring, but that it was loose—Beth knew that; Sara had shown Beth that it turned on her finger. It could have slipped off when Sara hadn't noticed. Jeremy had been taking chances all his life. He would consider getting away with Sara's ring a better-than-evens bet.

She had to go into Max's study to find the phone number of the club. If Max had been there she would not have told him because, right now, Jeremy was hers. Max could have him afterwards, anyone could have him afterwards, but first of all Sara was dealing with him herself.

Jeremy Bolton couldn't take a call at the moment, she was told, would she like to leave a message. That suited her because she had decided to go over and confront him. She said, 'Tell him Sara phoned and I'll be along.'

He'd know that she knew and it might panic him into getting rid of the ring, but he couldn't have had much chance so far. She would threaten him with Max and the law, and in her present mood of vengeful wrath she had no doubt she would be able to wipe the floor with him.

She could murder Jeremy, but she had to deal with him. She put a support bandage on to strengthen her ankle and pushed her flaming hair under a black velvet beret; she didn't want to look too conspicuous turning up at the Saddlers' Club. She told Mrs Thomson she was driving out to see a friend for about half an hour and went out to the garage and her BMW sports car. It was a smooth drive, there was not much strain on the ankle, and, being early evening, there was space for parking around the club.

Sara knew the club. She had been there before when she had been Sara Solway, but not often enough to be recognised by the large man in a tuxedo just inside the door or the striking blonde at the desk. But Jeremy had got her message and was expecting her, so she was ushered into the glitz and glitter, to a table behind one of the pillars.

Later the club would be crowded. There were empty tables now and no one on the tiny dance floor, but it was still a public place with a fair number of customers so she would have to keep the scene low-key. Quietly and forcibly she would tell Jeremy what she thought of him and what she would do to him if she did not get her ring back right now.

He was with her almost as soon as she was seated. He took another seat and asked, 'What's up, Sar?' looking straight into her face without a flicker of guilt. Jeremy could be a barefaced liar, but this was very good acting.

'You know what's up,' she said, and he shook his head. 'You took my ring.'

'What?' His mouth fell open.

'My diamond ring. It was on the dressing table when you were there and when you went it was gone.'

'Uh-uh.' Mouth still open, he shook his head again. 'Not me,' he said.

'There was no one else. And you were scared to death when you saw Max.'

'Max Vella scares me to death,' said Jeremy. 'He scares everybody to death. I'd just tried to borrow money from you so I was worried about him finding me with you. But I wouldn't take your ring, Sar, and I wouldn't lift anything out of his house for a fortune. Are you sure your ring's gone?'

'Of course I am.' She had been playing around, taking pieces out of jewellery boxes, putting them back again. She said, *'Yes.'*

'You're not sure, are you?' said Jeremy. 'How well have you looked for it?'

She had not searched at all. She had been so sure that he had taken it. 'It's the kind of thing you would do, isn't it?' she said, and he shrugged.

'Well, sometimes—not lately, though. If your ring's gone I know nothing about it.'

He met her eyes so steadily she was almost convinced. One of the ways she could tell when Jeremy was lying was that he always had difficulty meeting her eyes. She said, 'Maybe, just maybe, I'm misjudging you.'

Jeremy grinned, 'There's a first time for everything; I'd enjoy that.'

'So would I,' she said. 'I really hope I have.' She smiled wryly and Jeremy took her hand. The man who came round the pillar was bigger than the bouncer at the door, and Jeremy dropped Sara's hand as if it had become red-hot. 'What are you doing here?' Sara heard herself squeal.

'I own it,' said Max. 'But in this case I'm collecting my wife. Time to go home.'

Now she would have to try and explain what she was doing there. Outside the club, he said, 'We'll take my car; we don't want to put any more strain on the ankle.' That sounded ironic rather than considerate, but she got into the passenger seat beside him and when he turned towards her she shrank back instinctively.

He whipped off the black velvet hat and her red hair tumbled over her shoulders. 'Incognito?' he enquired, but when she opened her mouth he said, 'Be quiet.' She was not sure what the matter was now; why shouldn't she have driven out to the club? But Max's profile was grim enough to convince her that if she tried to talk she would be shut up again, so she sat beside him during a silent journey back to the Moated House.

And into the house. He took her arm when they got out of the car, still without saying a word. In

the hall he opened the first door, into the blue drawing room, and closed the door when they were both
inside the room, alone. Then Sara got in the first
word. 'You weren't there by accident, were you?
How did you know where I was?' But there had
been her phone call and her going off in her car,
perhaps a call from the club. His spies were everywhere. 'Forget it,' she said.

'Not this time,' he said. 'We're not talking about
a piece of porcelain now.' Don't worry about the
vase. Accidents happen… So what had happened
now that mattered more? Everybody's scared to
death of Max Vella, Jeremy had said. Sara had not
thought she was, but there was something intimi-
dating in his size and stillness when he was looming
over her as he was now. 'The question is,' he said,
'what were you doing at the club? Finishing this
afternoon's business with Bolton?'

'In a way, but—'

'Did he ask you for money this afternoon?'

'Well, yes, but—'

'You were taking him money?'

'*No.*'

'Why not?' He was giving her no chance to answer. 'You have money. You married money. All
that talk about your sister—was it keeping her husband out of jail that motivated you?'

He knew about this, and she said, 'Of course it
was; they were one and the same thing.'

'Hardly.' That puzzled her for a moment. 'There
is a difference between a sister and a lover,' he said,
and she couldn't speak; her mind was blown. He

went on, 'By marrying me you were saving him. Was he always your real concern? You two get on so well together that you must always have been fonder of him than you claimed. You must always have been very good friends indeed.'

She couldn't take in what she was hearing. It was so crazy, she should have been laughing. She sounded as if she was laughing when she said, 'I went to see him because I thought he'd pinched my ring.'

The scarred eyebrow rose quizzically and his voice was soft. 'And had he?'

'I—might have been mistaken.'

'It wouldn't be your first mistake. But when you thought he'd stolen your ring why didn't you tell me?'

'I wanted to handle it myself.'

'You didn't want me to hear about it. You thought he was thieving from you but you were still saving his skin. Very touching. And that was a charming scene in the club. You two looked as if you were made for each other.'

She didn't sound as if she was laughing now because her throat was numb, the words she was getting out were choking her. 'You actually believe that my sister's husband and I—?' She couldn't say it.

Max drawled, 'Were lovers? Why not? It's not that unusual.'

'You might not think so, but to me it's obscene.'

'I do have a vulgar mind at times. Put it down

to the life I lead.' He was almost smiling, a smile that chilled her.

She said bitterly, 'If Jeremy ran and I ran with him would you come hunting us both?'

He took no time to consider that. His answer was immediate, and scathing, 'You'd be in no danger; I've never considered forcing an unwilling woman.'

'That's nice to know,' she said. She got out of the room and went up to her bedroom. The brilliant was in her jewel box. So she had misjudged Jeremy; she had made another mistake. A small, unimportant mistake compared to the big ones.

She looked at the fabulous ring and remembered the saying about diamonds being the only ice that kept a woman warm. The diamonds were not comforting her. She was colder than she had been in the snowdrift, but after tonight they were the only warmth she was going to get in this marriage.

CHAPTER EIGHT

WHEN Max walked into the bedroom Sara tensed against what was coming next. When he said, 'Eight o'clock,' she stared.

'What?'

'We're eating at eight. It's a half-hour drive.'

'We're eating out together, after what just happened?'

He shrugged. 'Why not? Nothing has happened that makes that much difference. That you and Jeremy Bolton were lovers doesn't affect your efficiency as mistress of this house or your social standing as my wife. There'll be no scandal in the future; you'll have no opportunity for an affair and Bolton would never find the nerve.'

Sara was dazed. There was nothing she could say in answer to this, except that it was an appalling accusation and that Max could believe it was sickening. She said, 'You're wrong. But then you're the one who never makes mistakes—Douglas Druitt told me that—so it's not much use arguing, is it? Would you like me to move into another room?

'Not unless you want to give the gossip writers a field day,' he drawled, and she could imagine what would be written: Tycoon Max Vella and his very new wife have already moved into separate bedrooms…

In the dressing table mirror she looked at the reflection of their bed. He might have followed her eyes because he said, 'It's a very large bed. Equal to a couple of good-sized singles. You'd be as safe in there as in your own room with the door locked. I won't lay a finger on you. I find the idea of you lying back and thinking of Jeremy Bolton a total turn-off.' He sounded more bored than angry. 'Will you be ready at half past seven?'

She nodded. She couldn't speak, and she couldn't think how she could handle this. She changed and fixed her hair and her make-up, all the excitement she had felt at what was going to be a wonderful evening turned to ashes.

On the surface it was a pleasant evening—a new French restaurant with a famous chef. The food would have been delicious if she had had the slightest appetite. He talked about his other homes—the Spanish villa, an Irish castle, a London house and a yacht. Where would Sara like to go? She needed a holiday and she should be viewing the property.

The lifestyle as his wife was still hers. The contract still held with one clause deleted—he no longer desired her because he believed she and Jeremy had been lovers and she still hungered for Jeremy. And while he thought her capable of that she very surely did not want him possessing her.

He could be the sexiest man she had ever met.

He could turn her on so easily and so potently. But after this he would be making no sexual demands, and that way she could go on living with him, sharing his bed. For him there would always be other beds, other women…

Max went to his study when they came back to the house, and Sara was in the king-sized bed long before he joined her. That must have been in the early hours because she was asleep, and she had not fallen asleep easily. She woke next morning as he came out of the bathroom, a dark blue towel around his waist as if he had just stepped out of the shower. The phone was ringing and he went to answer it. She looked across at the broad shoulders and the rippling muscles of his back with a sleepy surge of longing, and then she remembered.

She could taste the bitterness like acid in her mouth. When he put down the phone and said, 'Good morning,' to her she felt so angry she could have spat at him. He had no proof because there was no proof, he was utterly mistaken, but she was too hurt to try to defend herself. She turned and pretended to sleep as he went into the dressing room and later came out and left the room.

Mrs Thomson brought tea in as Sara was dressing. 'I hear a lustre vase got broken,' she said. That was not the only thing to be smashed, Sara thought miserably.

Mrs Thomson was waiting to hear how, and Sara changed the subject by asking, 'Where's the orchid?' She had just noticed the box had gone, and it might get Mrs Thomson talking about something else.

It did get her talking, very quickly, that orchids had to be kept cool and it had been put in a fridge. Something about that flower was disturbing Mrs Thomson—she had taken it away—and Sara said, 'Do you know who sent it?'

'No, I don't.' Yes, you do, thought Sara.

'How about Imogen Swarbrick?' she said.

'I'm sure I don't know,' said Mrs Thomson. 'Whatever makes you think that?'

'I must be turning psychic,' Sara said, because she was suddenly not guessing, she was certain. Max knew who'd sent it, but Lucy who had brought it up to Sara did not. So why was Imogen sending her a flower?

Sara finished dressing and found Imogen's number. She was using the phone in the study, sitting in Max's chair behind his desk, not expecting Imogen to answer her own phone so that when the husky voice murmured, 'Who is it?' she drew in a quick breath.

'Sara; thank you for the orchid.'

'You liked it. I'm so pleased. They're my favourite. A friend sends them to me on—special occasions. I thought he wouldn't mind you having one.'

'Did he?' Sara asked, and Imogen laughed her throaty laugh.

'Well, yes, he did rather. But it's all right now;

things between us couldn't be better. How are you, Sara? Done any more riding in snowstorms?'

That was what Sara was doing now, galloping into a storm. 'We must get together,' said Imogen maliciously. 'We could have such a lovely, long talk.'

A long talk with Imogen would be absolute hell. Sara was shaking. She couldn't face the thought of the 'special occasions' being described to her. 'We must some time,' she said, and hung up. In future she would keep well clear of Imogen.

January was a bitterly cold month. Even indoors, with the central heating on and fires burning in all the big fireplaces, draughts seemed to lie in wait for Sara, coming at her unexpectedly and chilling her to the bone.

She had a full agenda that month. She went with Max to small dinner parties and to huge functions, to the ballet, to the opera, a couple of opening nights, a new play and revival of a musical. Everywhere they were treated like VIPs, and Sara was handling her solo role pretty well too.

Alison came in two mornings a week, always efficient, always reserved, helping Sara with her mail and her diary dates. Sara had been co-opted onto various charity committees and intended working hard for them.

There had to be those who knew how quickly the Vella marriage had turned platonic, but it was not general knowledge. None of Sara's family or friends knew that, although she and Max occasionally shared a bed, they had not slept together as lovers since before the New Year's Eve ball. When Imogen had put a hand on his arm and had said in that voice that made Sara's hackles rise, 'You should have remembered I always come back'.

If Max still believed, as he obviously did, that Sara was still carrying a torch for Jeremy he seemed to be too arrogant ever to consider competing. He had never been emotionally involved and in every other way Sara was proving a suitable and biddable partner.

That month Sara almost convinced herself that she was too busy to think of Imogen. Some nights Max was away from home on business, but he could have been with anyone. Other nights—more often than not now—he slept in the little room leading off his study. Sara didn't see him then, she couldn't really know where he was, but she would not let herself brood on that, and he was still treating her very well indeed.

He bolstered her confidence, telling her she looked good, telling her enough about the bigwigs she was meeting to make her smile and cut them right down to size in her eyes. Juicy bits of scandal the press had never got wind of. So there was still a bond between them, he was still supporting her, and not only financially, even if she thought he had replaced her sexually.

He still brought her gifts too. One was a Fabergé heart in blue enamel and gold, with a 'S' encrusted in diamonds. He could afford it, he was a collector of precious things, but when she took the heart out of the faded velvet box she wished it was how it had been in the beginning. So that instead of saying, 'Thank you, it's beautiful,' she could have kissed him and thanked him in another way.

Two days later Sara met Imogen again. It had to happen. She had expected to see her in any number of places. It was in a local dress shop where nothing carried a price tag and everything had a top designer label. Debbie, one of Sara's old friends, worked here as an assistant and phoned Sara when anything came in that she thought Sara would like. She knew Sara's style and got commission from her custom, and was always glad to find that Sara was as friendly and down-to-earth as she had been when she couldn't have afforded one of their scarves let alone a whole range of anything.

Sara was trying on a couple of dresses when the cubicle door swung open and Imogen sauntered in after her. 'I thought it was you,' said Imogen. 'The hair.' She leaned against the wall, arms folded. 'How are you? Have you got over the surprise yet?'

'What?'

'Max asking you to marry him.' Sara would always find that surprising, even after Douglas Druitt had tried to explain it to her. 'Shall I tell you why he did?' Imogen was almost whispering, her heart-shaped face sharp and malicious.

Sara said, 'No thanks.'

But Imogen whispered on, 'Because I turned him

down. He wanted to get married and I wouldn't be rushed and we got into an argument about it. I've had some thrilling rows with Max. Well for once I managed to knock his macho pride for six, because he picks you up from nowhere and marries you.'

Her voice was soft and venomous. 'And that must have surprised you, considering he'd never given you a second look before, let alone having a six-month affair. Because he was sleeping with me until a few days before he married you and I made sure he needed nobody else.'

An image of Max and Imogen making love together flashed into Sara's mind like forked lightning and she blacked it out, because she never let herself dwell on that. She asked, trying to sound bored, 'So why are you telling me this?'

'I wanted you to know.' The violet eyes were glowing; Imogen was enjoying herself, cruel as a cat with a mouse. 'You're having a lovely time now, but make hay while the sun shines because it is not going to last.' She touched the heavy silk folds of the dress. 'You won't come out of it too badly; Max is a generous man.'

She turned to go, then looked at Sara again. 'Pretty little thing, the Fabergé heart, and the "S" in diamonds. Sacha, perhaps? Or Sonia? Or what about "substitute"?'

Sara managed a choking laugh and knew that the little heart had been broken for her as surely as the lustre vase.

Both dresses were in her size. She took one without trying it on because she had to get out into the air, and Debbie went out of the shop with her to ask her, 'Is Imogen Swarbrick a friend of yours?'

'Yuk!' said Sara.

Debbie hissed, 'She is a bitch. Nothing's ever good enough for her. I can't think why she keeps coming in.'

Sara grinned, managing to fool Debbie that everything was fine with her. 'Next time she comes in make her a coffee and spike it with rat poison.'

When she got home Sara sat quietly for a while then she walked around the house. She really loved this house, she always had, and as Max's wife she belonged here. She was not being locked out because Imogen wanted her gone. She wanted Sara out of the picture, but Sara was not going quietly; she was not going at all.

She had an understanding with Max, a job of work in a way, and she would never get a better one. She was fiercely determined to hang onto it, and she went on, playing her part as mistress of the Moated House, until only a few days after her meeting with Imogen when she reached her own limit and everything changed for ever.

Her breakfast had been brought into the breakfast room with a couple of morning papers, and while she gulped coffee she opened a newspaper, scanning the headlines and turning pages. Until she reached the gossip page when she sat very still, holding the paper in whitening fingertips.

This was the paper that had broken the news of

the Vella elopement and of Sara riding in the snowstorm. Now there was a picture of Imogen, outside
a small hotel, kissing a man before getting into a
taxi. The man was Max; it was a good, clear shot.
The paragraph that went with it read:

Property tycoon Max Vella shares a tender moment with socialite Imogen Swarbrick after dinner *á deux* in one of London's more exclusive
hideaway hotels. No sign of Sara, Max's bride,
but neither Max nor Imogen seem to be missing
her…

Imogen's suit looked as if it was made of velvet,
and the flower she wore on the lapel was surely an
orchid, so this meeting had been a 'special occa-
sion'. As Sara stared at the picture it came alive, in
colour. She was seeing the purple velvet suit that
matched Imogen's eyes and the purple flower. She
could hear Imogen's laughter and smell the faint
tang of Max's aftershave. She could hear Max's
deep, slow voice, saying a brief goodbye to the
woman he had always wanted.

Mrs Thomson bustled into the room. She had just
heard what was on the gossip page, and was trying
to get the paper back before Sara saw it. Seeing the
page open, she said, 'You don't want to take any
notice of that. They'll print any sort of rubbish.'

'Thank you,' Sara said dismissively.

Mrs Thomson was sorry for Sara, who had been
shaping up nicely into a first-class mistress of the

household. But if she was going to tackle Max Vella over this she'd get no joy. He was master here.

This was one of Alison's mornings. Sara went to the small room they used as an office and there was Alison, waiting for Sara, waiting for trouble. Eyes hidden as always behind the big, dark glasses but with a worried frown between her brows. As Sara walked into the room she began, 'Look, you don't want—'

A phone rang. Alison picked it up, looking as if she was about to say 'No comment' when her expression changed and she held the receiver towards Sara. 'It's Max.'

'How's that for on cue?' Sara muttered. 'Hello,' she said.

Max said, 'We must talk.'

'What's to talk about?'

'Give me Alison,' he said.

She passed the phone back and heard him say, 'Keep her there.'

Alison's eyebrows went higher than her spectacles. She said, awe-struck, 'You wouldn't be walking out on him?'

'You are not going to believe this,' said Sara, 'Nobody will believe me, but I am walking. I don't want any of this.' Not even the house. Nothing.

Alison was gasping for breath. 'Because of a paparazzi shot? You should know that the press sensationalises everything—you used to be a reporter yourself.'

But this was Imogen, the woman Max wanted—which was the only thing Sara wanted to be.
And who was wearing an orchid for a special oc-
casion. 'Did you know about Imogen?' she asked,
and Alison shrugged.

'I knew she was around, but he married you.'

'We had a contract and now I want out.'

'You can't.'

'We'll see.'

'You'll wait till he gets here?'

Sara's smile was so wry it was no smile at all.
'Will he sack you if I don't?'

'No,' Alison said, flatly and fiercely. 'He's a
good boss, a good man. If you leave him you're a
crazy lady. I never have known what to make of
you. It had to be the money you needed, you and
your family, but couldn't you see what you were
getting in Max?'

All Alison's cool had gone. She was flushed and
furious. 'He's one in a million. You'll never find
another man to come near him. Did you see us, my
husband and me at the New Year's Eve party? That
was due to Max. It's a wonder Andrew can even
walk, let alone dance. A parachute jump went
wrong—a weekend club he used to belong to. Max
paid for operations, treatment, everything. Kept his
job open for him. Nobody was to be told, but everybody working for him knows he's a tower of
strength when you're in trouble. What's the *matter*
with you? Why are you *doing* this?'

Because I love him, Sara could have told her. So

terribly that I cannot live here with the agony of knowing he does not love me. But sooner or later she would have to face Max, and she said wearily, 'All right, I'll be here.'

'Good,' said Alison, her lips set, her jaw jutted. Sara almost smiled, thinking, She'd try to sit on me if I tried to leave. She liked Alison now, seeing her as a woman who could be a good friend.

She asked, 'Why do you always wear dark glasses?'

'Because I'm blind as a bat without them,' Alison snapped.

That was something they had in common. Sara must have been bat-blind herself not to have seen what was happening. That she was falling in love with a man she could die for. Impulsively she said, 'I need a drink. I know it's early, but I really could use a glass of champagne. Any chance of you joining me?'

'No chance,' said Alison. 'What's there to celebrate?'

There was nothing to celebrate, but Sara needed Dutch courage and anything else that might lift her just a little out of this black despair. She took a bottle of champagne up to her bedroom and spent a few minutes struggling with the foil and cork before the cork shot out and the wine foamed into a tumbler from the bathroom. She drank as if it were medicine, and it tasted bitter although it was from a vintage year.

She had no idea where she was going from

here—not to Beth's or her mother's, she couldn't begin to explain to them, and she might be an embarrassment to friends. To somewhere out of the way where she could lie low and try to get her head and her life together. A hideaway hotel like Max and Imogen had found, and the thought of that brought pain that even a tumbler of champagne hardly dulled.

She began dropping a few clothes into a case. She would miss her dolls' house. That tiny world had been good for escaping into. If he would ship the dolls' house to her some time she would be glad to have it. She pulled out her diamond earstuds and put them on the dressing table. Most of her jewellery was in a wall safe, some in cases in these drawers. She would be leaving all that behind, including the rings she was wearing now. Except her wedding ring. She would keep that but nothing else.

It would have been heartbreaking to say goodbye to Bess so she kept away from the stables. She paused in front of the black lacquered display cabinet containing the porcelain pair of Harlequin and Columbine, opened the glass door and took out the little ballerina that reminded her of Beth.

'How do you feel about joining a sister on the run?' she asked the figurine in her cupped hands. She might smuggle this out in her case. It would be spoiling another pair, following the lustre vases. But that would be the only sign that Sara, the nobody from nowhere had once lived here. Max might miss her for a little while but not enough to ask her to return, and that was why she must give him another reason for her leaving.

If she told him now, I love you, she could end up clinging to him, begging him to love her a little. She might not be able to stop herself begging and that would be a terrible memory to take away.

She was at the top of the main staircase when the door in the hall below opened and Max walked into the house. With him striding towards the foot of the stairs the silence shattered and the air seemed to crackle, as though a storm had come in with him. Sara took a few backward steps along the gallery, her free hand steadying her by gripping the balustrade, because suddenly her head was swimming and the champagne seemed a really stupid idea.

Reaching her, Max took her arm at the elbow and they passed doors until they reached the bedroom. She had left the door ajar. The case, open on the floor, would be the first thing he saw. And then the half-empty bottle and the glass on the rug beside it. She set the figurine on the nearest flat surface because her hands were trembling so badly she could hardly hold it. Then she turned to face Max.

He was absolutely still, she was shaking like a jerking marionette. 'I want to go away,' she said.

'I thought you might.'

He would know. 'You always know, don't you?' she said. 'Where I'm going, what I'm doing. When I saw Beth, when I went to the club. Your spies must be everywhere.'

'I don't have spies where you're concerned.'
Like heck, she thought. 'The club? I thought Bolton
would be after money, I thought you might be taking it to him, and I knew you'd see your sister the
first opportunity you got.'

That was reasonable. He understood her very
well. She said, 'You were half-right.'

'And now you want to go away. A holiday?'

That would get her out of here, make the break
easier. 'Yes,' she said.

'Because of this morning's paper?'

She was sobering as rapidly as if she had fallen
into icy water. It was not the champagne that was
making everything she said sound stupid. It was
because she couldn't tell him the truth that she was
floundering and blundering, 'Maybe the picture
triggered it. I know that part of your life is none of
my business, I know where my limits lie, I know
what's expected of me. But I don't really know you
at all, and I am realising that I am afraid of you.'

'What?'

She babbled on, 'I've never been absolutely sure
you saw me in the mirror and that you weren't getting rid of a business rival. You could have married
me to keep me quiet.' And got a look of utter disbelief.

'I think you must be much drunker than you
seem,' Max drawled. 'Do you know who I was talking to on bonfire night while you were doing your
hot reporter act?' She hadn't given the man with
the quiet and worried voice a second thought until

now. Now she shook her head, and he said, 'It was Harry. They've had that hotel on lease for twenty-odd years. The owners have decided to sell, and I was backing Harry. Does he strike you as a hit man?'

'Of course not.' Of course she had never believed there was a hit man.

'You don't know enough about me,' said Max harshly. 'What do you want to know? My family history?' She was standing with her back to the little table in the window, and she pressed her hands along the edge to support herself when he began to pace the room. 'I don't know much about that myself,' he said. 'I had parents once, poor but honest; he was a bank clerk, she was a housewife. They were orphans, they'd met in an orphanage. My father's parents could have been gipsies; he was as dark as I am. Is this what you're needing to know?'

He stopped pacing, to glare at her. 'Where do you think you're going?'

'I don't know where I'm going.' He was at the other side of the room and her voice was so strangled it could hardly have reached him.

'Not with Jeremy Bolton?' he said.

And her vocal cords cleared miraculously enough for her to bellow, 'Don't start that. Jeremy's always been more trouble than both the twins put together. He's never grown up; mentally he's about the same age as the twins. I wouldn't touch Jeremy with a barge pole even if he wasn't married to my sister.' She was glaring now. 'If he was the last man on earth and free as a bird I still wouldn't want him in a million years.'

'Why didn't you say so?' said Max.

'You made it pretty clear what you thought, and I did say so. I said that the idea was horrible, but it's more than horrible, it's hysterical.'

He said, 'That picture this morning. I was dining at that hotel—a business appointment—and Imogen turned up. It was not a meeting arranged by me. I never saw the photographer.'

'You just saw Imogen wearing an orchid? She told me they were her favourite flower. I rang her to thank her for the one she sent me and she said a very good friend gave them to her on special occasions.'

'I'll bet they do,' Max said.

'Not you?'

'Not for the last six months.' They moved no closer, but a glimmer of hope was getting brighter with every word.

'Imogen turns up here and there,' he said. 'Sending you that flaming orchid was typical; I could have wrung her neck over that.' It had been the orchid that had made him so angry, not the broken vase. 'But yesterday was the clincher. She had to have got in touch with the photographer and given him that crap about a tête á tête. She'd enjoy seeing that in print. She's not very bright; she can believe any publicity she wants to believe.'

Max was beside her now. He held out a hand and took her to the Chesterfield sofa. She sat, looking down at her hands in her lap. He sat, looking at her. 'Now,' he said. '*Why* are you going?'

If there was no Imogen anything was possible. The sure thing was that Sara was staying. She said in a small voice, with a burst of courage, 'I've slipped up on the small print of our contract because I started falling in love with you. And it hasn't stopped, it's got worse. I've got the awful example of my mother and Beth but it's happened to me with one difference—there was always another woman around for them. They lived with that but I couldn't. I said I could never commit murder but after seeing that picture I'm not sure any more.'

'Makes me glad I've explained it,' said Max.

She was nestling against him and it felt wonderful, feeling his strength and his kindness. She said, 'I'm sorry about falling in love with you; I won't be boring about it, but you've been so nice. Sometimes.' Her heart was going like a sledge-hammer. 'My dolls' house, Bess, the Fabergé with "S" for Sara.'

'For Sara of course.'

'Imogen said it was "S" for substitute. I met her last week and she told me she turned you down so you picked me up.'

'That sounds like Imogen.'

Half an hour ago she had believed she had lost everything that made life worth living. Now she was happier than she had ever been in her life, sitting here, talking, telling Max something that would make him smile. 'Douglas said he thought she'd put

the idea of marriage into your head and you'd decided you wanted a wife who would do as she was
told rather than a free spirit like Imogen.'

Max roared with laughter. 'You do what you're
told? Not always a very good judge of character, is
he, our Douglas? And do me a favour—stop asking
around why I wanted to marry you because no one
has a clue.'

He was going to tell her why, and she held her
breath. He said, 'I suppose Douglas was nearest.
Imogen wanted marriage, I didn't. I'd never considered it until— Remember the rockets going up?
The shooting star for wishing on if you could find
the right one? I thought then—and it came as quite
a surprise to me—this girl could be the one. The
more I saw of you, talked to you, the surer I was
that we would make a very good partnership.'

'So I got the contract?'

'It seemed a reasonable arrangement for both of
us, but I realised early on it was not going to be
that simple. During the marriage ceremony you
hesitated; I thought you were having second
thoughts. If you had turned to walk away I'd have
gone down on my knees to you; it mattered that
much that you became my wife.'

She was filled with tenderness, and her eyes with
tears. 'I love you,' she said softly. 'Why have you
always guarded against love?'

Suddenly his face was unreadable and his voice
sounded as if he was speaking from somewhere far
away. 'I was with my mother when she was killed

outright in a hit-and-run. I had broken bones, internal injuries, this.' He indicated the scarred eyebrow. 'All that mended, but a week after she died my father went away.'

'He left you?'

'For good. He hanged himself.' So that was why he had had no sympathy for Beth, who would have left the children as his father had done. Sara could not manage even a whisper, just a horrified breath. 'Oh, no…'

'It stayed with me—how vulnerable love makes you—so we were going to share everything but love. But I've always been scared of losing you because I knew I couldn't face a life where I never saw you again, never had the right to touch you, could never look round and find you smiling at me.'

He was seeing Sara now, coming back to her from a lonely place, and she went into his arms as close as she could, wrapping her own arms around him. She knew now how he had looked as a child, as a boy, as a younger man, all the faces behind the handsome, arrogant mask. As if they had always known each other, always been there for each other.

He buried his face in her hair. 'I couldn't make love to you; I was terrified you'd be thinking of Jeremy. I was jealous of Douglas too, that first night we were back. You had him eating out of your hand, you were listening to him when I wanted you to be looking at me. I didn't realise it was jealousy, but it put me in a foul mood.'

She said gaily, 'Oh, yes, I remember it well.'

'Do you know where I want to take you now?' Before she could say anything he lifted her in his arms and carried her the few long strides to the bed, laying her down on the soft, uncreased expanse of counterpane.

'Here?' She looked up with laughing eyes.

'What better place to take you?'

It was like a first love making. Shedding clothes was done as if for the first time. He touched her with wonder, running his hands over her smooth skin as though he was reassuring himself that she was here with him. They came together gently, lingering over each caress. She had lain naked in his arms before but he had never looked so heart-stoppingly handsome to her as he did now. 'I love you,' he said. 'Your taste.' He kissed her lightly, gently. 'Your smell.' He breathed in the aroma of her skin. 'Your temper. Beside you everyone else seems only half-alive.'

The miracle of it seized them then, sending their love making into a celebration so passionately triumphant that Sara felt fireworks should be exploding around them. Later she said, 'I love you.' She hardly had the strength to raise her head from his chest, but she managed to turn her head enough for her lips to shape the words.

The clock was ticking and her heart was pounding, and she thought of her family. 'Will it be all right for Beth and the twins?' she wondered.

'Sure to be.' He grinned. 'But I wouldn't bank on Jeremy's chances.'

'Who needs Jeremy!' She leaned over, her swathe of red hair tickling Max's face. He sat up and pulled her to him, laughing with her as, over his shoulder, she saw Columbine, high on points in her ballerina pose, perched on the edge of a tallboy, and yelped, 'She'll fall.'

'Who will?'

Sara shot off the bed and darted across the room. 'Columbine.'

On closer inspection the figurine seemed less precarious, but she set it safely back and began to explain to a puzzled Max, 'I was kidnapping her. I was leaving everything else.' Not the wedding ring; she could never have taken that off. 'But when I passed the cabinet it seemed a good idea to take her with me. I think she looks like Beth.'

'A little,' Max conceded. 'She's a pretty little thing. But Harlequin would have missed her. They've been inseparable for years.'

'I'll take her back to him.' She went back to Max. 'Sorry, Columbine. It had to be the champagne or I'd have known you didn't want to leave him.' She looked across towards the half-empty bottle on the rug. 'Medicinal,' she said. 'It tasted like medicine.'

'Really?' Now he got off the bed and she thought again how beautiful he was as she watched him fetch another glass and pour champagne into both glasses.

When she sipped this time it was delicious. 'Now it's absolutely perfect,' she said.

'Now everything is absolutely perfect.' He drank a little, watching her. He didn't need to tell her she was beautiful; she would always know that from the look of love in his eyes.

'Who shall we drink to?' she said. 'Absent friends?'

'Forget the absent friends. You're here. I'm here. Nobody else matters. To us.'

'To us,' she said, and they raised their glasses together, welcoming their wonderful future.

MILLS & BOON®

Next Month's Romances

♡

Each month you can choose from a wide variety of romance novels from Mills & Boon®. Below are the new titles to look out for next month from the Presents™ and Enchanted™ series.

Presents™

FANTASY FOR TWO	Penny Jordan
AN EXCELLENT WIFE?	Charlotte Lamb
FUGITIVE BRIDE	Miranda Lee
THE GROOM SAID MAYBE!	Sandra Marton
THE MILLIONAIRE'S BABY	Diana Hamilton
MAKE-OVER MARRIAGE	Sharon Kendrick
THE SECRET FATHER	Kim Lawrence
WHEN DRAGONS DREAM	Kathleen O'Brien

Enchanted™

BERESFORD'S BRIDE	Margaret Way
THE FAKE FIANCÉ!	Leigh Michaels
A WEDDING IN THE FAMILY	Susan Fox
INSTANT MOTHER	Emma Richmond
RACHEL AND THE TOUGH GUY	Jeanne Allan
ANOTHER CHANCE FOR DADDY	Patricia Knoll
FALLING FOR JACK	Trisha David
MARRY IN HASTE	Heather Allison

On sale from 4th May 1998

H1 9804

Available at most branches of
WH Smith, John Menzies, Martins, Tesco,
Asda, Volume One, Sainsbury and Safeway

SUSAN WIGGS

The Lightkeeper

Lighthouse keeper Jesse Morgan's reclusive life is
changed forever when he finds Mary Dare washed up on
the shore one morning—unconscious and pregnant.
She's keeping a secret—one that puts them both in
terrible danger.

*"A classic beauty and the beast love story...
A poignant, beautiful romance."*
—bestselling author Kristin Hannah

1-55166-301-5
AVAILABLE FROM MAY 1998

MIRA®

DEBBIE MACOMBER

The Playboy and the Widow

A confirmed bachelor, Cliff Howard wasn't prepared to
trade in the fast lane for car pools. Diana Collins lived life
hiding behind motherhood and determined to play it
safe. They were both adept at playing their roles.
Until the playboy met the widow...

"Debbie Macomber's stories sparkle with love and laughter..."
—*New York Times* bestselling author, Jayne Ann Krentz

1-55166-080-6
AVAILABLE FROM MAY 1998

MIRA®

DANCE FEVER

How would you like to win a year's supply of Mills & Boon® books? Well you can and they're FREE! Simply complete the competition below and send it to us by 31st October 1998. The first five correct entries picked after the closing date will each win a year's subscription to the Mills & Boon series of their choice. What could be easier?

OBLARMOL
AMBUR
RTOXTFO
RASQUE
GANCO

KOPLA
OOOOMTLCIN
MALOENCF
SITWT
LASSA

EVJI
TAZLW
ACHACH
SCDIO
MAABS

G	R	I	H	C	H	A	R	J	T	O	N
O	P	A	R	L	H	U	B	P	I	B	W
M	O	O	R	L	L	A	B	M	C	V	H
B	L	D	I	O	O	K	C	L	U	P	E
R	K	U	B	N	C	R	Q	H	V	R	Z
S	A	N	I	O	O	N	G	W	A	S	V
T	S	I	N	R	M	G	E	U	B	G	H
W	L	G	H	S	O	R	Q	M	M	B	L
I	A	P	N	O	T	S	L	R	A	H	C
S	S	L	U	K	I	A	S	F	S	L	S
T	O	R	T	X	O	F	O	X	T	R	F
G	U	I	P	Z	N	D	I	S	C	O	Q

D8C

Please turn over for details of how to enter ➪

HOW TO ENTER

There is a list of fifteen mixed up words overleaf, all of which when unscrambled spell popular dances. When you have unscrambled each word, you will find them hidden in the grid. They may appear forwards, backwards or diagonally. As you find each one, draw a line through it. Find all fifteen and fill in the coupon below then pop this page into an envelope and post it today. Don't forget you could win a year's supply of Mills & Boon® books—you don't even need to pay for a stamp!

Mills & Boon Dance Fever Competition
FREEPOST CN81, Croydon, Surrey, CR9 3WZ
EIRE readers send competition to PO Box 4546, Dublin 24.

Please tick the series you would like to receive if you are one of the lucky winners

Presents™ ❏   Enchanted™ ❏   Medical Romance™ ❏
Historical Romance™ ❏   Temptation® ❏

Are you a Reader Service™ subscriber?   Yes ❏   No ❏

Ms/Mrs/Miss/Mr ....Intials ....(BLOCK CAPITALS PLEASE)

Surname...

Address ....

....

....Postcode...........................

(I am over 18 years of age)   D8C

Closing date for entries is 31st October 1998.
One application per household. Competition open to residents of the UK and Ireland only. You may be mailed with offers from other reputable companies as a result of this application. If you would prefer not to receive such offers, please tick this box. ❏

Mills & Boon is a registered trademark of Harlequin Mills & Boon Ltd.